Dungeons, Dragons, and Buckaroos
A Select Your Own Timeline Adventure

CHUCK TINGLE

DEDICATION

For all who are not afraid to break out of their roles.

HOW TO READ THIS BOOK:

Welcome to The Tingleverse, a place where unicorns, bigfeet, dinosaurs and living objects are a typical part of our daily lives. This reality is similar to the one that you're currently reading from, but positioned on a slightly different timeline.

Every action you take, or don't take, creates several new timelines of reality. These worlds have been blossoming into existence since the universe began, and will continue until it ends. It's a power that we all have, but rarely know we're using.

This book will illustrate just how important making choices can be. Unlike most books, which are read chronologically from front to back, you read a Select Your Own Timeline book by following the instructions in italics at the bottom of most pages. If there is only one option, these words will inform you which page to turn to next. However, there will often be multiple choices that you, the reader, get to select on this important journey.

These forks in your journey will look similar to this:

To order the spaghetti, turn to page 1325
To order the chocolate milk, turn to page 7489
Leave the restaurant on page 3244

If there are no words in italics at the bottom of your page (or story ending), it is assumed you should continue reading onto the next chronological page of the book, as you normally would.

Throughout your Tingleverse journey, you will sometimes find an item that you can carry with you. It's important to remember the items you've collected, so using a piece of scrap paper to write them down as you go might be helpful, though not required. When you receive an item, it will be written in all capital letters LIKE THIS.

The only other time you will see something written plainly in all capital letters is if you reach the end of a particular timeline path, and thusly the end of your story. It will be written as THE END.

If you come to a path that explicitly involves an item you don't have, you cannot take this path. If you cannot remember whether or not you possess an item, then it's assumed you do not. In this case you lost your item or left it somewhere along your journey.

Sometimes, a specific path you take will cause you to lose an item. If an item is lost, it will be written in all capitals and italics, *LIKE THIS*. Sometimes, instead of a specific item, you will lose *ALL ITEMS* you are carrying (or other specific instructions).

If you ever return to the first page, you will automatically lose all of your items.

Now that we've covered all the rules, please enjoy your journey through the various timelines of The Tingleverse! Your tale begins on page one.

The stone cottage around you is rarely this lively, but right now the energy coursing through this room is crackling with excitement and adventure. You can feel your heart pounding out of your chest as you stare across the table at your friend, wondering what will happen next as he weaves his story of fantasy and adventure.

He's just described the most ruthless verbal attack from your boss, a suited man who hurls insults from behind his large desk and threatens to dock your pay if you're not careful. It's a frightening thing to imagine, a dystopian future several hundred years from now where horses have been replaced by mechanical steeds and arcane powers are available to everyone, resting in the palm of your hand. In this imaginary world you and your friends have created, there's no such thing as dragons or misplacer beasts, just the monotonous grind of working your life away in a tiny office cubicle.

You know it's ridiculous and it could never really happen. Someone would surely overthrow any king who took things that far, and there wouldn't be enough swords in the land to save them.

For now, though, you and your friends are happy to let this terrifying world run wild in your imaginations.

The game is simple enough. Your friend Galoran describes the scene, and you tell him what you do to interact with this fantastical description. To see if you accomplish these tasks, you roll multisided dice and calculate the outcome.

Your friends call it role-playing.

While you haven't left this round wooden table for hours, it feels as though you've enjoyed all kinds of incredible encounters with strange and unusual adversaries.

In the game world you've slept in and missed the call of your mechanical rooster (known as an alarm clock), but successfully snuck into work with some particularly lucky die rolls.

Unfortunately, your boss has caught you sneaking this month's financial reports into his office, and now you've gotta explain yourself.

Galoran gazes up at you from behind a thin wooden panel that divides the table between your friends and him. "Your boss is very upset," he begins, his eyes widening with enthusiasm. "The man's nostrils flare as he asks what the hell you're doing in his office."

"I tell him there was a last minute change to the reports. They're not actually late," you offer, thinking fast.

Galoran nods. "Alright, roll a fabrication check."

You look down at the parchment in front of you, searching through the statistics of your futuristic role-play character and eventually finding your lying and fabrication score."

The rest of your friends watch with nervous apprehension, recognizing a failure here could mean disaster for your entire party.

You rattle the die around in your hands just a little while longer, then toss it across your table with a loud clatter. Everyone holds their breath, leaning forward to witness the results.

A smile crosses your face as you see the number you've thrown, the highest score possible on this particular die. "Twenty," you read aloud.

Everyone cheers excitedly, but before you have a chance to relax there's a loud knock on your wooden cottage door. The real door.

You all freeze, turning curiously toward the sound.

"Who is it?" you call out.

"The king's guard!" comes a booming voice from the other side.

Your friends gasp as a cold chill courses through your veins. The king's guard are the most skilled and fearsome warriors in all the kingdom of Billings, trained from their youth to become ruthless killing machines who will stop at nothing in defense of King Rolo.

Slowly, you stand and approach the door, carefully unlocking it and pulling it open.

Two handsome velociraptors in heavy plate armor loom before you, large and imposing. They each carry hefty broadswords that hang from their belts.

"What's this about?" you question.

"You have been summoned by King Rolo," the muscular dinosaur informs you. "He requests your presence."

"Right now?" you ask, your voice quaking in fear.

"Right now," the velociraptor confirms.

You glance back at your friends, who look on with expressions of great concern and confusion.

"I guess you'll have to finish the game without me," you offer.

Without another word, you head out of your cottage and begin to follow the guards as they lead you up the cobblestone street toward a towering castle.

The kingdom of Billings is a grand, sprawling landscape of

thatched roofs and stone structures, overflowing with characters from all walks of life. A sentient lute sings and dances on a nearby corner, delighting onlookers with a show of juggling blades. Farther down, a parasaurolophus merchant hawks various treasures from faraway lands, including a massive dragon's claw.

Usually, you appreciate your walks through the city, but today your mind is elsewhere. You're scanning the recesses of your memory, struggling to remember anything you did to warrant such an unexpected request from the king.

Your mind continues to come up blank.

"I'm not... in trouble am I?" you finally question.

"I don't know," the guard replies. "Are you?"

You shake your head.

"This whole thing is very secretive," the other guard chimes in. "We're not even sure why we're picking you up, just that it's very important. The way I see it, that could mean one of two things. Either you're the chosen one, some kind of hero in the rough who's here to save us all... or you've done something so bad that your impending torture is too unspeakable to burden another soul with comprehending."

"Oh," you reply awkwardly.

"Don't you worry," the raptor continues. "That's a fifty-fifty chance at being one of the greats!"

You arrive at the central castle, passing a few more of the king's guards before heading inside. Soon enough, you're winding your way up a set of beautiful, ornate staircases, passing from one room to the next until you finally arrive at the king's chambers.

It's here, right outside the enormous double doors, that your dinosaur escorts stop.

"We have strict instructions to leave you here," one of the guards offers.

"I'm supposed to just head inside?" you question. "Alone with the king?"

"It's not my call," the velociraptor retorts. "It's Rolo's."

Not knowing what else to do, you push onward, stepping through the massive golden doors to find yourself in an enormous throne room. Large white pillars run the length of this chamber on either side, framing a huge crimson carpet that extends to the throne itself.

It's on this ornate throne that King Rolo sits, an enormous, sentient twenty-sided die like the kind you use for your role-playing games back at the cottage.

"Your highness," you blurt, bowing in the presence of this living die.

"It is I who should be bowing to you," he retorts, his voice echoing off the walls of this enormous oblong chamber. "Come closer so I can get a better look at you."

You do as you're told, slowly approaching the throne and taking in the mighty presence of this powerful royal figure.

"Who would've thought the fate of this entire kingdom would come down to one simple commoner," King Rolo observes in wonder and awe. "It's hard to believe, and frankly I was skeptical at first, but my advisors have convinced me. I understand what needs to be done. These lands are only getting worse as the dark slime creeps its way across hill and valley, turning friend into foe, and foe into something even worse."

"Dark slime?" you question.

The king nods, then pulls out a small glass jar and holds it up to you. Within this container a strange black substance churns and boils, so black that no light can escape. Small tentacles lash about from within, and a hard, crustacean-like claw taps against the glass in a disturbing rhythm.

"My advisors call it The Void," King Rolo explains. "I'd heard a legend of this toxic substance when I was a boy, but had considered it nothing more than a fable. Now, I understand the truth of the matter. This substance has started to infect the edges of our world, but every day it creeps closer and closer to the kingdom of Billings."

"That's terrifying," you offer in return, your eyes still glued to the bizarre substance held tight within the king's grip. "I'm sure you have a plan to stop it, though."

"I do," King Rolo retorts. "You."

You scoff. "But... I'm nobody."

King Rolo smiles. "That's not what the prophecy says. According to the ancient tomes, a great role-player will arrive to save us all, a citizen of Billings who will end these times of war and strife and push back against The Void, returning our world to its former glory."

"I mean... I do some role-playing," you offer.

King Rolo nods. "I'm aware. I'm not sure what your little games have to do with the journey ahead, but I trust the prophecy. You must stop the black ooze or our kingdom will collapse."

You nod, slowly accepting your place as the hero of this story.

"So where do I start?" you finally question.

"The prophecy states the great role-player will take one of three forms: a clever wizard, a fearsome warrior, or a stoic true buckaroo," the king explains.

"I'm none of those," you admit.

"Not yet," King Rolo replies. "Which one would you like to become?"

Take the path of the wizard's prophecy on page 56
Take the path of the warrior's prophecy on page 31
Take the path of the true buckaroo's prophecy on page 38

6

You walk briskly toward the guard, feigning a mischievous and excited smile. "Hey," you call out. "I'm new. Are you the only stegosaurus on castle gate duty during the evenings?"

"Who wants to know?" the dinosaur replies skeptically, her hand dangling low by the hilt of her sword.

"There's a very sexy bigfoot at the Thaco Tavern," you explain. "She said she's got a thing for the stegosaurus at the gate."

The dinosaur guard's expression softens a bit. "Me?"

You shrug. "I mean, that's why I asked. You certainly fit the description."

"And she's cute?" the stegosaurus continues.

"Honestly, breathtaking," you reply. "Go have a look for yourself. She's still down there having a glass of chocolate milk."

The stegosaurus laughs. "I wish. You know I can't leave my post."

"Unless you're relieved," I offer. "Don't worry, I'll cover for you. The Thaco Tavern isn't too far."

I can tell this dinosaur is deeply conflicted, weighing her options.

"Very, very cute," you repeat one last time.

Finally, the stegosaurus gives into temptation. "Alright, I'll be right back," she caves, hurrying off down the road. "I owe you one!"

You watch as the guard disappears, swallowed by the night and leaving you to stand before the castle's main gate. The second the coast is clear you spring into action, slipping back through and hurrying to the front doors of the castle.

Creep inside to page 89

"Okay, okay!" you finally offer, raising your hands in a sign of surrender.

You open up your bag and pull out your *TURN INTO FROG SCROLL* and your *WEB SCROLL*.

"These are valuable magic items," you offer, "but they're all I have."

You carefully hand the parchments over to the coblin leader, who snatches them out of your hand and begins curiously looking them over.

"Powerful!" she announces loudly to the others. "Powerful! Magic!"

The mob of sentient corn on the cobs immediately erupt in a fit of excited chatter, thrilled by the haul from this particular ambush.

The loss of these scrolls is truly unfortunate, but at the same time, you've never been more thankful to have a truly inconspicuous weapon by your side. Although the staff you wield is quite powerful, it appears to be nothing more than a well-crafted walking stick when it's not in use.

The coblins ignore it completely.

Soon enough, the sentient vegetables are parting and allowing you passage, making their way back into the forest as they prepare for their next ambush.

You continue onward, frustrated to lose your scrolls, but thankful to be alive.

Your journey pushes onward to page 17

"Dang!" comes a sharp voice that erupts through the warm depths of your slumber.

You sit up in bed, startled to find Chuck Tingle standing in the doorway of your stone temple bedroom. Birds are chirping gleefully outside while warm morning light streams through the window.

"Good morning, buckaroo," Chuck finally continues. "Are you ready to prove love is real?"

"Yeah," you reply, still a little groggy as you struggle to collect your senses. "I'm just trying to pull it together."

"That's good news, bud," Chuck offers in return. "Path of the true buckaroo is to pull all kinds of things together, of making something out of nothing. The Void is nothingness, so if you are pulling it together, you're already taking a stance against The Void."

"Oh, okay then," you reply, trying your best to follow along as you climb out of bed.

"Thing is, you're *already* creating a story," Chuck explains. "The story of your life is a very important artistic way."

"Thank you," you offer in return.

"No, thank *you*. Our timeline is so blessed to have you here, but your path of proving love goes beyond this layer of reality," the white robed figure continues. "Gotta go right to the source."

Your head is still buzzing from this morning's early wake-up call, and at this point you've finally given up on following along. You understand the basics of what Chuck is telling you, but there's a mental haze that keeps you from diving too deep. "I'm sorry, I don't understand," you finally admit.

"That's okay," Chuck continues. "The path of the true buckaroo takes time. If you want to see your story for what it really is, you've gotta work on your inner trot. Follow me."

With that, Chuck turns and exits the room.

You quickly stand up and follow your true buckaroo mentor through the temple, weaving down long stone hallways until finally emerging into the lush, thick forest.

You and Chuck are all alone, standing in the calm silence of the morning. The mysterious man points up into the woods, his gesture directing you toward a winding path that snakes its way over a nearby hillside.

"Follow that trail until you reach the grove of true sight," Chuck explains. "Once there, meditate."

These words hang in the air for a moment as you await further instructions, then gradually realize this is all you'll get. With a smile and a nod, Chuck turns and shuffles back into the temple.

"Oh," you blurt, watching him go. "Okay then."

With nothing else to do, you turn and begin trekking your way up the tree covered hill, pushing through massive ferns that have grown over the trail after years of neglect. It's clear this route isn't traveled very often.

After a good hour of hiking the trail finally ends, coming to rest in a small clearing at the top of a mount. The circular area is lined with massive stones, the boulders forming a natural platform where one could peacefully sit. It's on this platform the tree canopy parts just enough to provide a glorious view of an endless blue sky above.

You climb up onto the platform and sit down, crossing your legs and closing your eyes. During the hike to get here your head had been swimming with thoughts, overwhelmed by curious excitement for your new inward journey, but now is the time to put these inquiries to bed.

Now is the time to free yourself from the burdens of this reality and gaze into the possibilities of the next. You're no longer asking what if, but observing what is.

You inhale, then exhale, focusing on your breathing as you allow yourself to slip deeper into the moment.

Eventually, the landscape of your mind peels away any preconceived notions of existence, revealing the blank white canvas below. Your mind is now completely empty.

Something begins to materialize before you, drifting through the mental mist. There are four people sitting around a table, every one of them dressed in a fashion that is distinctly unlike your own. It reminds you of some strange, abstract future, a world similar to the one you dream about while role-playing.

"It's too meta!" one of them yells. "If you let them break the fourth wall like this it'll ruin the game."

"Why?" another person around the table jumps in. "You really think there should be limits on what *can* and *can't* happen in a fantasy world? That's the whole point of all this! Anything goes!"

"Not anything goes!" the original arguer cries out. "Why does a sword and sorcery character need to understand they're part of a role-playing game? How does that help with fantasy immersion? There are *rules!*"

The longer you listen to their argument, the more you find yourself drawn into this new layer of existence. You feel as though you're being pulled toward it, not just physically but mentally too. The white canvas on which this table once sat begins to slowly fill itself in, creating an underground dungeon that you somehow recognize as a basement.

There are colorful prints on the wall and you understand them as blacklight posters. You perceive a brilliant red lava lamp bubbling away.

This strange knowledge continues to flood your mind faster and faster, consuming you entirely. Eventually, the new world feels even more real than the one you left behind.

You recognize the people around this table as your dear friends, Sarah, Lorbo and Jorlin. The final figure in this group is you.

You breathe in deep, sitting up straight in your chair as if waking from a trance. Sarah notices your strange body language, flashing you an awkward glance, but Lorbo and Jorlin are too busy arguing to notice.

Sitting before you is a table full of pens, paper, books and dice. The game you're playing is Bad Boys and Buckaroos. *ALL ITEMS* from your previous life are gone.

"Are you kidding me?" Jorlin yells, so frustrated that he erupts from his chair in anger.

"I'm definitely *not* kidding you," Lorbo replies calmly, shaking his head. "Rules are rules, man. The creators of this game spent a lot of time balancing everything out so we could all have a good time. Forgive me for wanting to keep it that way."

"Do you know what the number one *rule* is in Bad Boys and Buckaroos?" Jorlin replies. "It's *have fun!*"

Lorbo rolls his eyes. "That's just what people say, what they actually mean is too have fun while you follow the other rules so everything is fair."

Jorlin throws his hands up in frustration. "Ugh!" he cries out. "That's it, I'm out of here."

Sarah, the Tingle Master who runs your game, is now forced to join the conversation. "Wait, where are you going?"

"For a walk," is all that Jorlin offers.

Your friend turns and storms up the stairs, stomping extra hard as he goes and slamming the basement door behind him.

An awkward silence follows, until finally Lorbo stands and heads up behind him. "Let's take five," is all that he says. "I'll be out back."

Once the two angry players have disappeared, the room plunges into an oppressive silence. Now it's just you and Sarah sitting across from one another.

It slowly begins to dawn on you what The Void really is, at least in the context of your other life. If this darkness is a manifestation of grand cosmic nothingness, then it will grow larger and larger the more Jorlin and Lorbo fight. This animosity is warping your game, tearing it apart from the inside out.

The kingdom of Billings isn't being threatened by magical beasts or fantastic monsters, it's being threatened by the harsh reality of potential non-existence. If you don't help your friends see eye to eye, this might be you last Bad Boys and Buckaroos session.

"What do you think?" Sarah asks, breaking your focus. "Should we follow the rules strictly to make it objectively fair, or is having fun more important than anything else?"

If you think the rules should be strictly followed turn to page 21
If you think having fun is the only thing that matters turn to page 161
If you want to strike a balance turn to page 203

You dive to the left, but the misplacer beast skillfully predicted your move and lands directly on top of you.

The creature is an enormous canine with jet black fur and sharp, gnashing teeth. It stands on four muscular legs and is approximately eight feet long, but the thing that's truly frightening about this ferocious creature are the two long tentacles that rise from either shoulder blade. These slithering appendages are incredibly powerful, used to slash and whip their prey, and feature spiked pads at the end of each fur-covered length.

Of course, this fearsome predator is more than just its physical presence. All misplacer beasts are humming with magical energy, an unseen force that constantly swirls around them and causes their opponents to misplace things.

Right now, however, the only thing you can really see are the monster's enormous jaws as they snap ravenously just inches away from your face. You're pushing back against the misplacer beast with all of your strength, struggling to keep it away from you while you calculate your next move.

You're tempted to reach for your sword, but worried you won't be able to keep this frightening canine at bay with a single hand.

Give it everything you've got and push the beast off on page 192
Go for your sword on page 202

Without a second thought you turn and run as fast as you can into the grass, ducking down to keep your head from breaking the surface of this endless yellow field.

Your breathing heavy, you focus on pumping your arms and legs to push deeper and deeper into this golden expanse. It's only now that you realize just how brutally your arm has been sliced, watching as the fresh blood trails along behind you.

You also discover the weight of the misplacer beast has done a number on your leg, slowing you down a bit as every movement brings another surge of deep, sharp pain.

You hear a blood-curdling howl ring out across the field, followed shortly by the tense cacophony of rustling grass. The creature is enormous, but stealthy, so the one thing you don't hear are any heavy paws slamming the ground as it races after you,. Still, you can *feel* it following close behind, sense this powerful hunter closing in on its wounded prey.

Suddenly, the misplacer beast erupts through the golden grass, not behind you, but from the side. It slams into your body with it's wide open jaws, knocking you off your feet as it clamps down tight and begins to tear.

You scream in horror as the yellow grass around you becomes a brilliant red.

THE END

"Sure," you reply warmly. "I could use a friend on this journey."

The bumblebeeholder's massive eye goes wide with excitement. "Really?"

"Yeah!" you continue, equally enthusiastic.

Your new friend buzzes around in a circle a few times and then returns to the conversation. "So where are we headed?"

You pull out your map and unfurl it for Amanda, tracing the road ahead and then ending at Count Storb's dark tower. The bumblebeeholder looks it over, then shakes her head from side to side.

"Oh no, you don't wanna go that way," she offers. "Just head straight through the forest over here, you'll show up *way* faster. Might even get the drop on whoever you're after."

"Whoa!" you blurt, very impressed as you roll up the map and tuck it away. "I'm already glad you're along for the trip!"

You set off with your new friend, trekking farther and farther West as the landscape shifts and changes. Soon enough, the road falls away as the wilds consume everything.

The most surprising thing about your adventure, however, is just how quick it is.

It's not long before this woodland setting becomes twisted and broken. The dark tower draws close, and the Voidal influence of this cursed monument has tainted the land for miles. You're surrounded by a natural swamp, but no frogs croak or crickets chirp.

There is something wrong with this place, a sickness that permeates through everything.

Soon, the tower begins to loom before you and Amanda, rising into the sky in an affront to all that is good. The building is a twisting black spire, reaching out toward a gloomy haze above and reflecting off the dark swamp water below.

"So there's a dark sorcerer in there and we need to stop him?" the bumblebeeholder clarifies.

"Yep," you offer with a nod.

"So fun!" Amanda cries out, doing a quick backflip through the air.

As you approach the front doors, you feel a powerful necromantic energy emanating from within. The powers of The Void are strong here, something much mightier than life or death. Instead, you sense a profound nothingness that threatens to swallow everything.

You hesitate before heading through, focusing on the task at hand. Count Storb is in here somewhere, and it's up to you to stop him.

Finally, you push through and head inside, greeted by an enormous gothic foyer with high ceilings and a large spiral staircase meandering up from the other side of the room.

The place is exceptionally spooky, with torches lining the walls and cobwebs dangling everywhere. A huge, dust covered chandelier hangs from the ceiling, its candles lit and flickering.

You creep further into the building, making it halfway into this main hall before the door slams shut behind you. You jump in alarm, then laugh as you realize this unexpected sound is nothing more than the wind.

Gradually, however, a different unexpected noise begins to fill the hallway.

You listen carefully, struggling to figure out what's coming down the staircase and then gasping aloud when you see them.

A handful of zombies emerge from the darkness, staggering toward you with their arms outstretched. They're living objects, torn and tattered sheets of paper with a variety of numbers and letters scrawled out in organized columns. It appears they've been written on, then erased over and over again, this process repeating until they've developed holes running from one side to the other.

Along the top of these pages, the words 'character sheet' are written.

The paper zombies continue to stagger toward you, drawing closer with every passing second.

You ready your staff, preparing for battle when suddenly a powerful yellow beam of light erupts from behind you. You watch as it sweeps across the room, washing over the zombies and utterly vaporizing them in seconds.

The room falls back into silence as you glance over at Amanda, who doesn't seem to be aware of the amazing feat she just accomplished.

"Oh my god," you blurt. "You killed everyone!"

"I thought that was the point," the bumblebeeholder offers.

"Yeah, but..." you stammer. "I thought there was gonna be some kind of fight."

Count Storb emerges at the top of the staircase, creeping down with curious hesitance. He glances around the room, utterly confused.

"Uh... where are my character sheet zombies?"

"I guess they're dead," you offer in return. "Was that your whole clan?"

The count is an ominous stegosaurus in a long black clock, and you can tell he's accustomed to frightening others with his presence alone. Now, he just seems lost.

"Hey, do you wanna just turn yourself in?" you call over.

This comment manifests the exact opposite reaction to the one you were hoping for. The dark sorcerer immediately centers himself and regains his composure, offended by the suggestion of surrender.

"Never!" the dinosaur cries.

"Then prepare yourself," you roar, hoisting your staff into the air for added drama as it crackles with raw arcane energy, "for bat-"

Before you have a chance the finish your sentence, the bumblebeeholder blasts Count Storb with another magic bolt, turning him to dust in a brilliant flash of yellow.

You stand in silence for a moment.

"We did it!" Amanda blurts, buzzing around the foyer in celebration.

"That was… unexpected," you stammer. "You're very powerful."

The creature buzzes over, hovering before you and smiling wide. "I am?" she questions.

You nod.

"We should take out another sorcerer!" Amanda shouts. "Can we?"

"Uh... it's not really about that," you offer. "Count Storb was bad news, but the darkness has been defeated now. You don't need to vaporize anyone."

"Oh come on! You're no fun!" the bumblebeeholder cries out. "There's a town on the edge of the swamp! Let's go turn them to dust!"

Before you have a chance to stop her, Amanda swivels around and buzzes outside, disintegrating the front door to clear a path.

Talk some sense into Amanda on page 61

Attack her on page 130

If you have the 'turn into frog' scroll, use it to stop Amanda on page 26

Join her and destroy the town on page 107

If you have the honeysuckle candies, offer them to Amanda on page 79

You continue trekking farther and farther West, the landscape gradually shifting and changing as the road falls away and the wilds consume everything. Your journey is long and difficult, and a variety of frightening obstacles block your path, but somehow you manage to overcome every encounter.

With every step you can feel your wizardly power growing, the experiences of your quest shaping you into something more powerful than you could've ever imagined. While you continue to learn, you are no longer a novice in your arcane craft.

You finally feel like a hero.

Eventually, the natural setting begins to melt away, becoming twisted and broken as you find yourself in a particularly unique landscape. The dark tower draws close, and the Voidal influence of this cursed monument has tainted the land for miles. You are surrounded by a bubbling swamp, but no frogs croak or crickets chirp.

There is something wrong with this place, a sickness that permeates everything.

Soon, the tower begins to loom before you, rising up into the sky in an affront to all that is good. The building is a twisting black spire, reaching out toward a gloomy haze above and reflecting off the dark swamp water below.

As you approach the front doors, you sense a powerful necromantic energy emanating from within. The forces of The Void are strong here, something much more powerful than life or death. Instead, you sense a profound nothingness that threatens to swallow everything.

You hesitate before heading though, focusing on the task at hand. Count Storb is somewhere inside, and it's up to you to stop him.

Finally, you push open the enormous double doors and head through, greeted by an enormous gothic foyer with high ceilings and a large spiral staircase twisting up from the other side of the room.

The place is exceptionally spooky, with torches lining the walls and cobwebs dangling everywhere. A huge, dust covered chandelier hangs from the ceiling, it's candles lit and flickering.

You creep further into the building, making it halfway into this main foyer before the door slams shut behind you. You jump in alarm, then laugh as you realize this unexpected sound is nothing more than the wind.

Gradually, however, a different unexpected noise begins to fill the

18

hallway.

You listen carefully, struggling to figure out what's coming down the staircase and then gasping aloud when you see them.

A handful of zombies emerge from the darkness, staggering toward you with their arms outstretched. They're living objects, torn and tattered sheets of paper marked by a variety of numbers and letters in organized columns. It appears they've been written on and then erased over and over again, this process repeating until they've developed holes that go from one side to the other.

Along the top of these pages, the words 'character sheet' are written.

The paper zombies continue to stagger toward you, drawing closer with every passing second.

If you have the blue staff, fight them off on page 72
If you have the orange staff, fight them off on page 41
If you have the web scroll, use it on page 81
If you have the 'turn into frog' scroll, use it on page 36

"I can deal with the troll," you announce confidently.

Lady Norbalo cracks a smile, suddenly going from deeply annoyed to vaguely amused by your confidence. After the king plucked from obscurity to save Billings by way of sword and shield, it's easy to see why this unicorn would have trouble taking you seriously. Now, however, she seems to appreciate the fact that you're willing to try.

It's not nearly enough to *respect* you just yet, but at least she's not downright hostile.

Lady Norbalo presents you with a DAGGER.

"Take this," she offers. "You'll need it."

You accept the blade, then turn and make your way down to the castle basement. The whole time you find yourself trembling with anxiety, glancing down at the tiny dagger in your hand and wondering if it's nearly enough to take on a dungeon troll.

Eventually, you arrive at a large iron door in the castle basement. There are two guards standing watch and they greet you coldly.

"So you're the big bad warrior everyone's talking about?" one of the guards offers.

"I mean... I'm still in training," you reply awkwardly.

The guards exchange glances before one of them reaches out and opens the massive iron door for you. "Welcome to the castle dungeon," he offers. "Your troll is deep down in the older section, the part of the dungeon that's no longer used. Poke around long enough and you'll probably find him."

"You'll need this," the other castle guard offers, handing you a dungeon key. "It works on any dungeon lock. Go down the first set of stairs and walk the prisoner's hallway. At the end there's another door that leads to the older section."

"Thank you," you offer.

Soon enough, you're descending a long flight of stairs, the iron door closing behind you and plummeting this scene into an eerie quiet. You can hear screams and groans echoing in some far off torture chamber, but these close quarters are surprisingly still.

The ground levels out and presents you with a long stone hallway that's lined with iron-barred cells on either side. You creep your way along, peeking within these empty chambers by way of flickering torchlight.

As you reach the final cell a figure emerges from the shadows within, startling you. It's an old twenty-sided die, the same living object type as King Rolo, but one who's clearly taken a different path in life. They look worn and tired, any spark of color drained from their muted grey exterior.

"Help," the sentient die moans. "I've been framed."

You stop for a moment, staring at the living object. "I'm sure everyone down here says the same thing," you offer in return.

"It's the truth," the sentient twenty-sided die continues. "I've been thrown in dice jail for landing on too many critical misses, but whose fault is that? I'm just a die, I'm totally random! Is it really fair to sentence me to death?"

"I'm sorry, I've got a mission to take care of," you stammer. "I'm not your jury."

"There *was* no jury!" the die replies. "Just an angry player who rolled too many ones!"

You have trouble understanding exactly what he's talking about, but the emotional weight of this living die's pleas hits you just the same.

"Just open the lock and keep going," the die begs. "I'll do the rest to get myself out of here."

While this emotional plea has certainly tugged on your heart strings, you can't shake the fact this living object could easily be lying about how he ended up in his cell. You find yourself torn about what to do next.

Open the cell on page 177

Continue deeper into the dungeon on page 70

You consider this for a moment, weighing the question in your mind.

Sure, having fun is important, but without the strict framework of gameplay there'd be nothing to enjoy in the first place. Rules are there for a reason, and without them everything just falls apart.

"I really think we need to play with strict guidelines," you finally offer in return. "The rules are paramount."

Sarah's expression flickers slightly as you say this, but she maintains a smile. She's trying to listen with an open mind, but there's no question she disagrees with your sentiment.

Your friend is working something over in the depths of her mind, sorting through her beliefs as she synthesizes an appropriate response. She takes a deep breath and then slowly lets it out, as though finally accepting a fact that's been weighing her down for a very, very long time.

"I have to admit, I haven't had much fun being the Tingle Master lately," she offers.

"Oh," you blurt, a little surprised. "Really? The game seemed pretty fun, we just talked to the king and set out on a quest. It's getting good!"

Sarah just shakes her head. "Yeah, I know. I'm glad you all like the storyline, but it's still pretty exhausting for me to sort through all these rules *and* patch up debates between the group."

"Do you want someone else to be the Tingle Master?" you question. "I could run the game if you want."

"I don't think so," Sarah replies solemnly. "I think I'm just… done for a while."

Your friend stands up and gathers her books and dice. At first you think to protest, but you can already tell she's made up her mind.

This may be the session that finally got to Sarah, but it appears she's been considering this exit for a while.

Soon enough, you're the only one left at the table.

In the dim light of the basement, you suddenly feel incredibly lonely. This new world isn't nearly as fun as you'd hoped, and it quickly occurs to you that the best option is heading back into the fantasy realm from which you came.

No matter how hard you try, however, you can't seem to return.

"Focus," you tell yourself, closing your eyes tight. "Just remember where you *really* are. You're meditating in a clearing."

22

Of course, deep down you're not so sure. Are you actually meditating? Or is this new reality the one you truly belong to.

When you open your eyes, you're still sitting at a table in your friend's dimly lit basement.

Regardless of whether or not you belong on this reality, it looks like you're gonna be here for a while.

The future awaits on page 37

"Alright," you finally agree. "I'm in."

Darba smiles and nods. "Very well, your training begins now."

The next several weeks are spent under the care and tutelage of the sneak's guild, an underground organization that thrives in the nooks and crannies of this enormous kingdom. While the citizens of Billings go about their business, you are tasked with various training exercises that often push well past the edge of criminality.

You steal, bribe, trick, and most of all *sneak,* but through all of this you make sure to return what you've taken. While the sneak's guild have no problem with these morally dubious exercises, you make it very clear that you're here for one reason and one reason only: to fulfill the prophecy.

Regardless, this training is hard work. On your first few tasks you're caught red-handed and forced to run from the city guards, barely escaping with your life, but as the days wear on your skills become more and more refined. You learn to blend in with your surroundings, the dark shadows that once gave you pause now welcoming you as a friend.

During this time you also learn, and what your studies reveal is something you could've never expected.

King Rolo is not the kind soul that your previous interactions had lead you to believe. The king is correct in his confidence that a great evil is sweeping across the land, but this dark force is not quite what he makes it out to be.

The evil creeping through Billings is, in fact, brought on by the king himself. It is his overwhelming greed.

King Rolo has been syphoning off money from the subjects of Billings for years, slowly raising taxes and finding any number of unethical means to procure more and more wealth. Of course, the citizens of this land are none the wiser, but the sneaks' guild has all the evidence you could ask for.

Now it's time to turn the tables and bring peace and fairness back to Billings.

King Rolo has a vault tucked away within his chambers. Inside this vault is an incredible assortment of gold coin and priceless jewels, all of which the king has collected through immoral means. As the great role-player, your mission is to sneak into the castle and steal this treasure back, then distribute it to the good people of Billings in the dead of night.

You've been equipped with a magic bag that can hold anything you choose to place within it, allowing you to load up the king's treasure and make your escape. You've also been given a castle guard's uniform.

Now, on the evening of the big heist, you stake out the castle nervously. You're all done up in your stolen uniform, watching as a young stegosaurus stands at attention near the front gate.

Your talk is to convincingly relieve her of the duty, causing her to walk away from her post while you take the guard's place.

You take a deep breath, centering yourself and focusing on your training, then approach the dinosaur. There are two methods of manipulation you've been considering, but now is the moment to pick the best one.

You call out to the guard.

To exclaim "there's been an accident with a family member!" turn to page 151
To say "a beautiful unicorn at the inn was talking about you" turn to page 6

You circle the dragon slowly, watching its movements intently as you plan your attack. Eventually, the creature makes its move, snapping it's head toward you and opening its jaws wide for a ferocious bite. It's at this exact moment that you strike out with all the force you can muster, aiming straight for the creature's huge black eye.

It's a direct hit.

The dragon lets out a furious squeal, reeling back as it struggles to collect itself. The monster staggers from side to side, knocking over bottles of milk as it blindly fumbles around.

Go for the other eye on page 163
Go for the belly on page 158
Go for the heart on page 86

You quickly realize there's no way you're taking down Amanda in a head to head battle of raw magical force. You need to be smart about this, to hit her with something so powerful it stops the fight before it even starts.

Fortunately, you have just the thing.

You hurry after the bumblebeeholder, pulling the scroll out of your bag as you go and reading it at a full gallop while you trudge through the swamp. You let the incantation spill off your tongue in a cascade of strange mystical syllables.

Amanda, who's been flying way ahead, slows down a bit and then circles back in confusion. "What's going on?" she calls out.

You can't stop now.

"Hey!" the bumblebeeholder cries, spotting the scroll in your hands.

A surge of green crackling rings has started to bloom around you, growing in size then launching toward Amanda before she has a chance to react. The creature cries out, swooping awkwardly as her body rapidly shrinks and mutates. Seconds later, she plops into the swamp below as a tiny, frightened frog.

"Oh shit!" you blurt, realizing this the perfect place to lose track of her.

You hurry over and scoop up the amphibian, tucking her safely away in your bag and breathing a long sigh of relief.

It's been three years since that fateful day, but you still think about it often. You still see yourself as a wizard in training, your mind trudging forward in a never-ending pursuit for knowledge, but there's no question you were a novice back then.

You chuckle to yourself, leaning back in your chair as you take a break from the spell you're crafting. You're racking your mind, sorting through all the potential arcane components that might provide the desired effect.

Suddenly, it hits you.

"Honey!" you say aloud, snapping your fingers and climbing out of your chair.

You make your way through the hut, pushing outside and taking in the fresh evening air. Your cottage is positioned on the edge of the woods, and from here you can see the ever growing city of Billings in the distance.

Years ago, constructing a home this far out would be too unsafe, Voidal monsters roaming the land with sharp teeth and hungry bellies. Fortunately, you put a stop to that.

You walk around to the side of your hut where several bee boxes sit, humming with life and full of honey. You cast a quick skin protection spell then open the lid.

As you reach inside to break off a piece of honeycomb, you see a little green frog living happily with all the bees. They don't sting the amphibian, just welcome this creature as one of their own.

You smile, then close the lid and head back inside.

THE END

"I'm sorry, I can't help you," you offer, shaking your head and continuing on your way.

While this mysterious figure's offer is certainly interesting, it just doesn't seem like the path you were meant for. Besides, while the dark underbelly of this kingdom likely holds its fair share of adventure, it's also a place that's crawling with betrayal and deception. For all you know, this whole thing could've been a trap that's just been narrowly avoided.

You wander onward, sauntering over to a fruit stand and admiring some of the delicious options that have been gathered and displayed before you. There are all kinds of colorful edibles to choose from, and your mouth is already starting to water as you consider purchasing a quick snack.

"Excuse me!" comes a gruff voice from behind you, breaking your concentration.

You turn to find two large, hulking figures. They're city guards, dressed to the nines in sturdy plate armor and sporting disappointed frowns across their chiseled faces.

"You stole from a market stall back there," the lead guard states firmly.

You can't help but scoff. "What? I did *no* such thing."

"I suppose you don't mind if we check for candlesticks then?" the guard continues.

Before you have a chance to reply he reaches behind you and grabs something long and metallic out of your back pocket. You gasp aloud when you see it, a shining silver candlestick.

"What?" you cry out. "That's not mine!"

The next thing you know, the guards are upon you, wrestling you to the ground as you struggle to push them away. You fight back as valiantly as you can, but the next then you know a sharp crack rings out and the world plunges into utter darkness.

You float here in the endless abyss for a while, then eventually find yourself reconnecting with the physical realm. You slowly open your eyes, groggy and discombobulated as the world comes back into focus.

You're somewhere cold and dark, the location dimly lit by a series of flickering torches that line the far wall. Between you and the rest of this small room is a series of thick bars that extend from the floor to the ceiling, restricting your exit.

You're in the castle dungeon.

"Hello?" you call out, your voice echoing up and down the empty stone corridor beyond.

You hear someone's distant cries in return, but the longer you listen, the more you think these are simply the screams of someone being tortured, not a direct response to your initial shout.

You reach up and feel the back of your head, a large bump starting to grow where you'd been struck by the butt of someone's broadsword.

"Still not sure if this is your path?" a voice questions from the shadows.

You glance up to see a familiar figure approach, the unicorn from the market who you'd already declined to follow. This time, however, it appears your choices are a little more limited.

"Get me out of here!" you blurt, standing up and approaching the bars.

The unicorn smiles. "I can get you out just as easily as I put you in. If you're willing to come with me and fulfill the prophecy, then freedom is yours."

You now realize the unicorn planted a candlestick on you, and while you'd love to get the hell out of this dungeon, getting framed for theft doesn't exactly turn you into a thrilled collaborator.

Decline the unicorn's proposal on page 225
Go with the unicorn on page 172

After eyeing the chandelier chain you finally decide to let the dark sorcerer have his speech. Despite zoning out through most of it, you can tell he's been working on this thing for a long time, and it feels wrong to just cut him off like that.

More importantly, there's no telling if this little chandelier trap will actually work. For all you know, unfurling the chain could do nothing but trigger a safety mechanism and stop the chandelier in its tracks.

"Which you will not be able to stop!" the Count Storb yells, coming to the climax of his story. "Now that you're heard my plan, you can see why there's no way out of this puzzle I've constructed. You are trapped like a rat!"

You shake your head. "I've gotta be honest, I stopped listening halfway through."

The dinosaur narrows his eyes, first confused and then frustrated. "But... I spent a very long time putting the hero who comes to fulfill this prophecy in a very difficult ethical position. The choice you must now make is excruciating."

"Yeah, I didn't hear it," you offer.

Count Storb is growing increasingly heated now, his blood boiling over at the casual way you've brushed past his devious master plan.

"Then you... must... die!" the stegosaurus sorcerer cries out, charging toward you.

If you have the 'turn into frog' scroll use it on page 101
Fight with your staff on page 135

You let the king's question linger for a while, rolling these options over in your head and considering which one of the bunch you most connect with. At first brush all three of them seemed like a tall order for a common peasant of Billings like yourself, but upon further consideration, one begins to shimmer and sparkle within your mind.

You find yourself pulling away at first, some inner voice refusing to accept this heroic path could truly be a possible.

There must be some kind of mistake, the inner voice insists.

The draw of your heroic path refuses to give, however, standing tall and proud and demanding your attention. The more solid your visions of this potential future get, the more that inner voice of denial slowly fades away and disappears.

"I choose the warrior path," you announce proudly.

King Rolo raises his eyebrow a bit. "Are you... sure?"

"Of course I'm sure!" you blurt, disappointed the reaction wasn't more supportive.

"Alright, alright," the king finally confirms with a nod. "Who am I to question the great prophecy? Wait... I'm the king. I can do whatever I want. But, I'll *choose* not to question the great prophecy."

"Thank you, your highness," you reply.

"This may be a grand path, but you're still only at the beginning," King Rolo continues. "I'm sending you to train with the kingdom's greatest knight, Lady Norbalo.

King Rolo raps his knuckles three times against the arm of his throne, these cracks echoing out through the chamber around you.

Immediately, the doors open and a tall, powerful knight strolls in with breathtaking confidence. She's a light orange unicorn with a long flowing mane. Her head is the only thing not covered by thick, heavy armor.

"Where is the chosen one?" Lady Norbalo calls out. "I'm excited to get started with our training!"

This mighty unicorn arrives before the throne, bowing for the king as she stands next to you. She has yet to acknowledge your presence.

"This is the chosen one," King Rolo offers, motioning in your direction.

Lady Norbalo turns to look, laughing as though the king is making some hilarious joke then faltering when she realizes he's being serious. You notice her disapproval bubbling up for a moment, threatening to break out in a verbal disagreement with the king before she pulls back. Finally, she settles in and accepts her fate.

"Yes, your highness," Lady Norbalo offers, bowing to the king and turning back toward you. "Follow me."

"Good luck!" King Rolo calls out as you and Lady Norbalo make your leave, exiting the chamber and heading down one of the long castle hallways.

The second you're out of earshot Lady Norbalo turns to you with a furious anger in her eyes. "Listen here, I don't know what you're trying to pull, but you are clearly not the chosen one. Can you even *lift* a sword?"

"Yeah," you insist. "I mean... I think so."

The unicorn shakes her head. "You couldn't even clear the troll out of the dungeon, let alone save our kingdom."

A spark of dissent suddenly flares up within you. "If it's so easy to clear out the troll, why haven't *you* done it?" you question.

Lady Norbalo is shocked by your counter, her expression quickly transitioning from anger to humored amusement. "It's below my paygrade," she finally offers, "but now that we've brought it up, maybe there's something to this. If you really want to train with me, then your first mission is simple. Rid the dungeon of that hideous troll and come back when you're finished."

Accept your mission on page 19
Decline and find a new path on page 78

Returning victorious to Lady Norbalo is a surreal experience, and as someone who typically imagines themselves in the role of a hero, you absolutely love this new taste of the real thing. At first, the unicorn warrior doesn't know what to think, but when you show her the lock of troll hair you procured on your first mission, her opinion is swayed.

Gradually, her skepticism begins to fade. The two of you embark on a rigorous training routine, working from sunrise to sunset in an effort to hone your skills and turn you into the ferocious warrior you're destined to be.

The days stretch into weeks, and soon enough you begin to wonder if and when this vigorous training will come to an end. Eventually, however, you arrive at the barracks to find that Lady Norbalo is waiting for you without her traditional armor and sword.

Today, she is dressed as a citizen of Billings, nothing more.

"What's going on?" you question, approaching the unicorn in confusion. "Are we not working today?"

"*You* are," Lady Norbalo offers with a knowing smile. "Today is my first day off in a long, long time."

It takes a moment for you to finally understand what she's saying, but when you realize what this means you immediately feel a wave of reverence and gratitude wash over you.

"Thank you for your training and guidance," you offer, dropping to one knee and bowing before the unicorn.

Lady Norbalo laughs. "You're welcome, but now is not the time for bows," she offers. "You have quite the walk ahead of you."

"Where am I going?" you question.

"As you know, The Void is sweeping its way across the land, infecting our world and creating monsters the likes of which Billings has never seen. Every passing day this darkness creeps closer to our kingdom," the unicorn explains in a solemn, serious tone. "As a warrior, I've trained you to cut to the heart of the matter, to take the most direct route. It is my belief the power of The Void is centered on the most powerful creature it has infected. Slay *that* creature, and the rest of this cosmic darkness will retreat back to the timeline from which it oozed forth."

"And what creature might that be?" you ask.

"There is a dragon in the distant mountains," Lady Norbalo continues. "Thanks to The Void, it now oozes with the toxic energy of the abyss. It is enormous and powerful, but I believe you have the training to bring it down."

"Yes, Lady Norbalo," you reply with a nod, accepting your mission.

"Do you still have the dagger I gave you at the beginning of your training?" the unicorn questions.

If you don't have the dagger turn to page 187
If you have the dagger turn to page 218

Soon enough, you're heading out through the city gates, finding yourself in the beautiful rolling fields of yellow grass that surround Billings. The sight is absolutely majestic, and although you've taken in this landscape plenty of times before, you can't help but give this glorious golden vision some extra weight within your mind. The adventure that lies ahead of you is a treacherous one, and there's a good chance you may never see these fields again.

According to Grimble the Grey's map, the dark tower is due West, which means you'll enjoy the comfort of this dirt road below your feet for quite some time. Unfortunately, the longer you travel along this path, the less maintained it becomes. You gradually stop seeing other friendly travelers as civilization drifts away and thick woods spring up around you.

As the trees loom higher and higher, the sun creeps its way across the sky. You walk for hours, watching as your path becomes a rugged, rock-covered trail.

You're all alone out here, and while that realization is a little frightening, it's also better than finding yourself in the presence of someone unsavory. For now, all alone is just fine.

As the sun begins its descent, however, something changes in the air. You get the distinct impression you're being watched from the bushes ahead, someone or *something* tracking your movements and anticipating your arrival.

It feels like someone is watching you.

Run forward and get through it quick on page 208
Turn back and return quietly through the bushes on page 113
Ignore the rustling on page 87

As the tattered zombie character sheets close in you decide to take your 'turn into frog' scroll for a spin. You pull out the parchment, quickly reading over the incantation as magical energy erupts before you.

Green sparks begin to crackle and leap from arcane rings what swirl around your body, growing in size until, eventually, they blast forth and strike on of the zombies.

The paper immediately transforms, shrinking down into a tiny frog that begins to hop around the foyer.

Unfortunately, your attention has been so focused on taking down a single zombie character sheet, you haven't been paying enough attention to the others. By the time you regain your focus, the undead pages are already upon you.

You raise your staff to take a swing at one of them, but by the time this weapon is above your head the undead pages are pulling you to the ground. You begin to scream as the zombie's tear into your flesh, pulling you apart and eating you alive.

THE END

As the years pass you think about your role-playing days less and less, those epic quests of sword and sorcery gradually dissolving within the depths of your memory bank. As new events come and go, these fantastic tales are pushed to the side and discarded piece by piece.

It would certainly be sad if you noticed it happening, but this erosion of long nights in the basement rolling dice and imagining monsters slips away without much fanfare. It's hard to miss something when you've forgotten how much it meant to you in the first place.

Every once in a while, however, something will strike you just right and your mind will open again, flooded with visions of medieval adventure. Sometimes it's a name, or a phrase, or a random image you catch sight of as you sit on the computer at work waiting for the new quarterly reports to load.

In this particular case you were shown an advertisement for an Alaskan cruise from Borson Reems Cruise Lines, and while the deep dark forests of this online ad aren't *precisely* the woods that filled your imagination on those epic journeys, it's close enough to spark something deep within.

Soon enough, you're leaning back in your chair and gazing at the stark white ceiling above your cubicle, a smile crossing your face as you remember that time you crept through the wilderness and discovered a mystical true buckaroo temple.

"What are you thinking about?" a voice blurts, breaking your concentration and causing you to abruptly sit up straight.

It's your friend Ashley, a curious co-worker who's stumbled upon one of your rare fantasy realm daydreams.

Unfortunately, Ashley is technically your superior here at the office, and you're not sure if telling her what's on your mind is the best idea. Your zone out was on company time.

Say you were thinking about fantasy tabletop role-playing games on page 84
Claim you were thinking about some work reports on page 152

"The path of the wizard and the warrior seem pretty fun," you finally offer, "but all that fighting is a little much for me. I'm happy to help save the kingdom, but if I can do it through deep stoic thought that's probably the best option."

King Rolo just stares for a moment, clearly surprised by your decision.

"Oh," the sentient die finally offers, nodding along. "Okay then, I guess this is a different kind of adventure."

"Did you... want me to fight a bunch of monsters?" you question awkwardly.

The king shrugs, trying to play it off. "No, no, it's fine. This isn't my prophecy, it's yours."

You can tell King Rolo is still a little disappointed with your decision, but at least he's doing his best to play along and make you feel comfortable with the choice. Despite his other shortcomings, the king appears to trust in this process.

"In that case, your journey begins at the true buckaroo temple," King Rolo finally continues, centering his focus once again. "You'll head out through the main city gate, then across the fields and into the wilderness. The true buckaroo temple is not easy to find, but if your heart is pure then the *temple* will find you. Ask for Chuck Tingle."

"Thank you, King Rolo," you reply, bowing deeply then turning to head out of the throne room.

While the direction of your journey feels right, it's hard not to second guess this decision as you make your way out of the castle. With every step you draw farther and farther away from the comfort and luxury of a straightforward story, drifting farther and farther into the abstract.

How can you help heal this world without a sword or a wand? Will the path of a stoic true buckaroo really hold sway over the mighty darkness of the endless cosmic Void as it creeps through your reality.

Only time will tell, but admitting the truth of your nervous apprehension seems like a reasonable start on this inner quest.

You stroll through the main gates of the city, greeted by endless fields of tall golden grass that seem to roll on and on forever. It's a glorious sight to behold, and although you've spent plenty of days out here before, this moment is something new.

There's a direction to your story now, a desire to show that the forces of love can overcome anything. While it's something you've always known, this is your moment to prove it.

Eventually, the yellow plains and farmland gives way to the edge of a deep, lush forest. It's here that you need your wits about you, a place where monsters of the wild are free to do their hunting. While you don't expect to encounter any Voidal creatures just yet, there are still plenty of natural beasts who would love to have you as a meal.

"Hey there, Buckaroo," comes a voice through the dark forest, causing you to jump in alarm.

You glance over to see a man in white robes and a pink bag over his head, the words 'love is real' scrawled across his brow. He's sitting on a log, calm and relaxed as he sips from a canteen.

"Are you Chuck Tingle?" you question.

"Dang! How'd you know, bud?" Chuck asks.

"King Rolo sent me to find you," you offer in return. "I'm the great role-player, from the prophecy."

The strange man stands up and shuffles over to you, walking around you twice as he looks you up and down. "Do you feel like the great role-player?" he questions.

You consider Chuck's words for a moment. "I'm not sure. I mean, this morning I was just another citizen of Billings, now the fate of the world rests on my shoulders. That's a lot of power."

"Well, if it makes you feel any less heckin' stressed then you should know *everyone* has this power," the mysterious man explains. "Every action that we take creates infinite other timelines. This happens for each moment as you trot through your reality and it makes you so mighty it's hard to even think about. Question is, what are you gonna use this power for? When those other timelines split off are they gonna be better or worse?"

"Better," you reply confidently.

"That's the true buckaroo way," Chuck offers with a smile, patting you on the shoulder. "I think you're definitely cut out for this."

With that, the man in the white robes and pink bag motions for you to follow, then starts making his way deeper into the woods.

The two of you venture into this humming natural landscape of old-growth trees and thick carpets of soft green moss. Light shines through the scene in warm hazy shafts that illuminate a dim, canopied world. As you travel, it's difficult to remember this is actually a very dangerous place.

It's just so beautiful.

The longer you walk, the more the sun begins to creep its way across the sky. Soon enough, warm afternoon air transitions into the cool chill of the evening.

Eventually, the soft drone of chanting voices begins to echo out through the woods, growing louder with every step as a large stone temple comes into view. There are figures all over the structure, going about their business in service of some unknown mystical tradition. A few of them are hugging warmly while others carry supplies to and from the temple.

As you pass these robed true buckaroos they stop what they're doing and turn to greet you warmly.

"Love is real!" they offer.

"Love is real," you instinctively retort, prompting kind smiles from the crowd.

You head inside the temple and Chuck Tingle leads you to a small chamber, featuring a single window and a modest bed.

"Hiked a long way, buckaroo," the mysterious man offers. "You should get some rest. Big day tomorrow, bright and early we'll trot and prove love. That's when the journey really begins."

With that, Chuck leaves.

His observation was dead on, you're absolutely exhausted. You climb into bed and within a few minutes you've drifted off to sleep, curious what the next morning will bring.

Wake up on page 8

You raise your staff and spring into action, rushing into the fray with your crackling orange weapon and tearing into these undead character sheets.

One of the zombies lurches toward you from the right, slow and steady as their mouth hangs open and a deep groan spills forth. You swing your staff like a bat, walloping them so hard they erupt in a sparkling explosion of orange energy.

Two more zombies approach from the left, and you quickly dispatch them with a similar treatment.

As the horde closes in you only become more skilled with your weapon, drawing on your training and manifesting incredible displays of arcane energy. The magical bolts are erupting from your staff like flaming arrows, tearing through the zombies in huge swaths.

Soon enough, these undead creatures are completely destroyed and the floor is littered with character sheet scraps.

You gaze across the foyer as the dark sorcerer appears before you, a stegosaurus in a long black cloak at the top of the staircase.

"The prophecy is a fool's errand," the dinosaur bellows. "My magic is too powerful to succumb to the promises of some ancient wishful thinking. This world belongs to The Void now."

"Not if I can help it!" you call back, ready for battle.

"Ha! A novice wizard like yourself?" the sorcerer calls back, strolling confidently down the stairs and slowly making their way toward you with a menacing swagger. "I've been studying the dark arts for centuries, and The Void has only amplified my powers! My training started before you were born!"

The dinosaur keeps talking, but by now you've tuned out their meandering, overblown villain speech. Instead, you're focused on the next step in your battle plan.

You suddenly notice Storb is standing directly under the enormous hanging chandelier, and the chain that holds it aloft is connected to the wall right next to you.

Let him finish his speech on page 30
Drop the chandelier on page 45

42

As you head down the stairs of the wizard's tower you can't help but wonder if you've made the right decision. A deadly mission of might and magic would be a hell of a way to pass the time, but the thought of partaking in that much death and destruction puts a bad taste in your mouth that you just can't ignore.

The way of the true buckaroo, however, sounds more than a little intriguing. These stoic and meditative scholars live on the outskirts of society, journeying through the depths of their mind instead of trekking to the edge of the physical world.

Their powers of focus and wisdom are the stuff of legends, and although putting yourself into that position is quite intimidating, you'll never know unless you give it a shot.

Soon enough, you're strolling out through the main gate of the city, greeted by endless fields of tall golden grass that seem to roll on and on forever. It's a glorious sight to behold, and although you've spent plenty of days out here before, this moment is something new.

There's a direction to your story now, a quest to prove the forces of love can overcome anything that stands in their way. While it's something you've always known, this is your moment to actually stand up and prove it.

Eventually, the yellow plains and farmland gives way to the edge of a deep, lush forest. It's here that you need your wits about you, a place where the monsters of the wilds are free to creep along and do their hunting. While you don't expect any Voidal creatures just yet, there are still plenty of natural beasts who would love to have you as a meal.

"Hey there, buckaroo," comes a voice through the dark forest, causing you to jump in alarm.

You glance over to see a man in white robes with a pink bag over his head, the words 'love is real' scrawled over his brow. He's sitting on a log, calm and relaxed as he sips from a canteen.

"Oh, hey," you reply, startled. "Are you one of the true buckaroos?"

"Yes! Dang! How'd you know, bud?" Chuck asks.

"A wizard told me I could find you out here," you offer in return. "I'm the great role-player, from the prophecy."

The strange man stands up and shuffles over to you, walking around you twice as he looks you up and down. "Do you *feel* like the great role-player?" he questions.

You consider Chuck's words for a moment. "I'm not sure. I mean, this morning I was just another citizen of Billings, now the fate of the world rests on my shoulders. That's a lot of power."

"Well, if it makes you feel any less heckin' stressed then you should know *everyone* has this power," the mysterious man explains. "Every action that we take creates infinite other timelines. This happens for each moment as you trot through your reality and it makes you so mighty it's hard to even think about. Question is, what are you gonna use this power for? When those other timelines split off are they gonna be better or worse?"

"Better," you reply confidently.

"That's the true buckaroo way," Chuck offers with a smile, patting you on the shoulder. "I think you're definitely cut out for this."

With that, the man in the white robes and pink bag motions for you to follow, then starts making his way deeper into the woods.

The two of you venture into this humming natural landscape of old-growth trees and thick carpets of soft green moss. Light shines through the scene in warm hazy shafts that illuminate a dim, canopied world. As you travel, it's difficult to remember this is actually a very dangerous place.

It's just so beautiful.

The longer you walk, the more the sun begins to creep its way across the sky. Soon enough, warm afternoon air transitions into the cool chill of the evening.

Eventually, the soft drone of chanting voices begins to echo out through the woods, growing louder with every step as a large stone temple comes into view. There are figures all over the structure, going about their business in service of some unknown mystical tradition. A few of them are hugging warmly while others carry supplies to and from the temple.

As you pass these robed true buckaroos they stop what they're doing and turn to greet you warmly.

"Love is real!" they offer.

"Love is real," you instinctively retort, prompting kind smiles from the crowd.

You head inside the temple and Chuck Tingle leads you to a small chamber, featuring a single window and a modest bed.

"Hiked a long way, buckaroo," the mysterious man offers. "You should get some rest. Big day tomorrow, bright and early we'll trot and prove love. That's when the journey really begins."

      With that, Chuck leaves.

      His observation was dead on, you're absolutely exhausted. You climb into bed and within a few minutes you've drifted off to sleep, curious what the next morning will bring.

Wake up on page 8

This dark sorcerer certainly loves the sound of his own voice, and he hasn't stopped rambling as you consider your options on how to proceed. The dinosaur is so caught up in telling you how powerful he is, that he barely notices as you reach out and unfurl the tightly wrapped chain next to you.

Suddenly, the cable whips upward as a chandelier comes crashing down, this massive, metal contraption crushing the dark sorcerer under its incredible weight.

You stand in silence for a moment, half expecting him to emerge from the rubble in some even more terrifying form, but this second coming never arrives. Looks like Storb wasn't quite as powerful as he thought.

The dark tower around you slowly begins to change, the Void's mighty hold finally loosening as the color returns to this beautiful structure. What was once strange and terrifying is now flooding with warmth.

The fire begins to subside, caught fast enough to be driven back by this arcane cleansing.

You smile, satisfied with a job well done.

You're just about to leave when a new figure emerges from the shadows, their presence stopping you in your tracks. It's a light purple unicorn with a sparkling horn, clad in the soft leather attire of the thieves and rogues that call this vast world home. You can immediately tell this unicorn is a certified sneak, creeping through the darkness and living on the fringe of society.

"Nicely done," he offers.

You ready your staff, prepared for battle with your unexpected visitor.

"Whoa, whoa, whoa," the unicorn blurts, showing their hands. "I'm not here to fight, I'm here to ask for help."

"I just got done helping," you reply. "I've fulfilled the prophecy."

The unicorn thief laughs. "I'm sure King Rolo will be thrilled to know that you bought his story. The thing is, his interpretation of the prophecy couldn't be farther from the truth. The real villain here is the king himself, a greed-fueled ruler who flagrantly steals from the citizen of Billings."

You narrow your eyes, struggling to make sense of this new perspective. The unicorn doesn't strike you as a liar, but you can never be too careful.

"You *are* the chosen one, but not in the way you think," the unicorn continues. "Come with me a fulfill the real prophecy to bring light and love across this kingdom once again."

You're pretty exhausted after the completion of this epic quest, so starting another mission so quickly sounds like a real pain. However, if this sneak is telling the truth then maybe it's worth helping out.

Go with the unicorn on page 169
Decline and head home to page 96

You leap to the right and narrowly avoid this snarling, ferocious misplacer beast.

The creature is an enormous canine with jet black fur and sharp, gnashing teeth. It stands on four muscular legs and is approximately eight feet long, but the thing that's truly frightening about this creature are the two long tentacles that rise from either shoulder blade. These slithering appendages are incredibly powerful, used to slash and whip their prey, and feature spiked pads at the end of their fur-covered length.

Of course, this fearsome predator is more than just its physical presence. All misplacer beasts are humming with magical energy, an unseen force that constantly swirls around them and causes their opponents to misplace things.

Fortunately, as you reach back and grasp the hilt of your magic blade you discover the only thing misplaced this afternoon is your lunch. You center yourself, remembering your training as you circle the beast and wait for its approach. Your eyes are trained on its tentacles as they whip the air before you, testing your reaction time.

Suddenly, the creature snarls and charges forward, lashing out with a single tentacle and following with a bite from its enormous jaws.

You're ready. As the long furry appendage shoots in your direction you pull your sword from its sheathe, lashing out and slicing the tentacle clean off. Next, you roll to the side, allowing the misplacer beast you drive past you as you take a second swipe with your magic blade.

The creature lets out a howl of agony. You've slashed it down the middle, the beast's insides spilling forth as it collapses to the ground in a bloody heap.

You wipe the viscera from your sword and watch as your weapon's blue glow begins to shift and change. It appears the magical energy coursing through this blade is directly tethered to your own skill as a warrior, and after this encounter your technique has only improved.

To your amazement, the *BLUE SWORD* transforms into an ORANGE SWORD, your weapon overflowing with arcane energy.

You take a moment to collect yourself, then resume your journey.

Your quest continues on page 76

There's something exciting about the mysterious nature of this unicorn's offer, and it's enough to coax you along behind him. You're well aware thieves and rogues are not the trustworthy type, but in this particular case you're willing to take your chances.

After all, if there really *is* some prophecy with your face attached, you're curious to see how this underground mission compares to King Rolo's initial assignments.

Soon enough, you've arrived at the massive, looming city wall, this structure of defensive stonework towering over you. Guards patrol the top, but they're too high to pay much attention to you and your unicorn friend as you creep through the shadows.

You eventually arrive at a large boulder that pushed against the wall's base. The unicorn gazes up, timing his movements perfectly so the patrolling guards have their backs turned in perfect unison. Once the coast is clear, he rolls this boulder to the side and reveals a small hole, just big enough for the two of you to slip inside.

The next thing you know, you and your sneak companion are creeping along the inner foundations of Billings, a network of tunnels that weave through and below this sprawling kingdom.

"Just a little farther," the unicorn keeps assuring you, but with every new chamber it seems your goal is no closer to arrival.

Deeper and deeper you venture into this underground labyrinth, until finally your companion pushes away a hanging tarp and reveals a large stone chamber.

There are six figures sitting around a table in this dimly lit room, but when they catch sight of your arrival they all stand and scurry into the shadows. Now, only one entity remains at the central chair, eyeing you skeptically.

The woman is flat a square, a sentient book with the name "The Complete Guide To Sneaks" written in gold letters across her maroon cover. In smaller print, the words "Second edition" can be found, but you have no idea what this could possibly mean. Her corners are worn and scuffed after more adventures than you can imagine.

"Who the hell is this?" the sentient book questions, rolling up a map on the table before her and quickly putting it away.

"You don't recognize them?" your unicorn companion questions.

The living book narrows her eyes, taking you in with slightly closer scrutiny.

Quickly, the unicorn hurries over and gingerly opens her to a page in the middle, peeking within and then glancing back toward you. Your companion does this several times before closing the volume. "Yep, this is the one."

The sentient book's eyes go wide. "The prophecy!" she blurts, then motions for you to come sit across from her.

You do as you're told, pulling out a wooden chair and settling in directly across from this mysterious figure. All the others, including your new unicorn friend, disappear into the shadows.

"I'm Darba, headmaster of the sneaks' guild," the sentient book informs you. "Your face is one that many of our members recognize, written deep within my pages."

You nod along, listening intently.

"While the main tomes of lore have prophecies of their own, I'm what you would call *supplemental material,*" the sentient book explains. "I have a prophecy of my own, said to bring joy and peace to this land once again. Unlike the others, this prophecy is not just for those who dwell on the surface."

"What is it?" you question, cutting to the point. "What do you need me to do?"

Darba nods, appreciating your frankness. "You need to steal something from King Rolo," she finally reveals.

Your heart skips a beat, and the living book immediately notices your hesitance.

"Please understand, we'll be forced to kill you if you say no," she continues "The secrets of the sneaks' guild cannot leave this chamber."

Accept the mission on page 23
Decline the mission on page 224

"Actually, I *do* have a few items you can take," you admit. You open up your bag, moving very slowly so as not to alert the coblins.

"Give!" the leader shouts, extending her hand toward you in a demanding gesture.

"Of course," you continue, pulling forth the web scroll. "First, let me explain what this is."

You unfurl the parchment, gazing down at these magical instructions.

"This is a pretty dangerous item," you inform the mob of coblins that surrounds you. "With a single word you can capture an entire group in a sticky, magic web."

"Give!" the coblin leader repeats, growing impatient.

"Hold on, hold on," you retort. "It's quite simple really, all you need to say is... *spideralis webendron!*"

The second these words leave your lips a brilliant flash erupts from the web scroll. The document immediately turns to dust, falling through your fingers in a fine grey mist, but the manifestation it created is much more impressive.

Every single coblin has found themselves suck in a sticky web, like that of a spider only vastly larger. They are absolutely covered in this thick substance, held in place and shrieking in frustration.

"While I'd love to stay and chat, I've gotta be going," you offer the howling creatures. "I'm sure some rangers patrolling these woods will find you and clean up this mess."

You creep carefully over the scattered webs and the coblins trapped within, ready to continue on your way and then stopping abruptly when something catches your eye. It appears one of the coblins has a piece of delicious HONEYSUCKLE CANDY in their pocket.

You reach down and take the sweet snack for yourself, deciding it's the least they could offer after threatening your life.

You take a bite, then safe the rest for later.

"Thanks for the treat!" you call back over your shoulder, ready to hit the road.

It's only then you notice a single coblin has wiggled free of his webbing. The sentient corn is now sprinting off into the woods as fast as he can.

Chase the coblin to page 144
Chase the coblin to page 144
Let the coblin escape and keep traveling to page 201

You show up to Limber's house as night falls, a vast assortment of rulebooks and dice filling your bag as you make your way up the front walk. You've decided to arrive a little early, hoping to get things in order before the others make their appearance, but to your surprise the driveway is already full of cars.

You knock twice and the door flies open, Limber greeting you with a smile and a warm hug. She's still quiet, but you can tell her comfort is growing.

The house is simmering with energy, the whole gang already here and seated around a table in Limber's dining room. They're chatting away, helping themselves to an assortment of pregame snacks while they trade notes about each other's freshly crafted characters.

"Whoa," you blurt. "Looks like everyone is ready to play."

"When you said we could start building our characters before the session I got a little excited," Gorb admits. "Looks like everyone else had the same idea."

You can already tell this group is going to be a blast.

You sit down at the table and pull out your books, stacking them next to you. Shortly after comes the Tingle Master screen, a thin piece of foldable cardboard that keeps the others from looking at your notes, and last is a handful of dice.

You gaze out at your friends as they settle in, the air buzzing with anticipation.

You've only acted as the Tingle Master a few times before, but you're thrilled to find yourself in this important position. You get to set the stage, to make the fantasy world bloom around your players with well-crafted descriptions and tantalizing storylines.

While most games of Bad Boys and Buckaroos start in a chocolate milk tavern, you've decided to jump right into the action, dropping your characters in a spooky graveyard.

"The moon hangs high above, illuminating rows and rows of crumbling tombstones that stretch out in every direction," you begin.

As you craft the scene, the walls of the dining room begin to fall away, revealing a frightening cemetery complete with a rusted iron fence and low lying fog. You and the players are all standing in your medieval armor, ready for action.

"What's that?" Limber suddenly offers, breaking through the

silence and pointing through the mist.

A lantern slowly makes its way toward you, floating in the darkness and causing a sharp chill to run down your spine. The players draw their weapons, readying for battle as the tension builds and then immediately relaxing when an old, friendly gravedigger comes into view.

"A group of adventurers I see," the gravedigger offers. "I'm sorry I startled you, but I'm not the one you have to worry about. This cemetery is crawling with rickety living bicycle zombies."

"Bicycle zombies?" Gorb questions. "Sounds like something we might be able to help you with."

Soon enough, the gravedigger has recruited your friends to clear this area of the undead menace. Meanwhile, you decide to hang back a moment, enjoying the ambiance of this fantasy world that you've been denied for so long. You're the Tingle Master anyway, so ultimately this is *their* adventure, not yours.

Soon enough, you're left on your own to stroll through the cemetery and examine this fun and frightening setting.

"Hey there, buckaroo," comes a familiar voice.

You glance over to see Chuck Tingle sitting on one of the graves, waving happily as you approach your old friend.

"Chuck!" you shout. "I can't believe it's you!"

"I'm just so dang glad you found your way back," the true buckaroo offers. "Even though this is a scary place, it's not a *real* threat. The Void is nowhere to be found because the power of imagination is strong in this world! It's all thanks to you, bud!"

It's only then you notice the three graves that surround Chuck, gasping when you read the headstones.

The names of your old player group are carved deep into the stone, a marker for each one of them.

"Sarah, Jorlin and Lorbo," you read aloud, a profound sadness in your voice. "The original game is all here. It's great to start something new like this, but I miss them a lot."

"It's a fantasy world, bud," Chuck reminds you. "They could always come back."

You laugh. "I don't know if it's gonna matter this time," you offer in return. "They left out there, not in here."

"These worlds are more connected than you know," Chuck Tingle retorts from behind his pink mask. "If you made a *really dang good* roll, you could probably bring them back."

Chuck reaches out a drops a twenty-sided die into your palm.

"What do you say, buckaroo?" Chuck offers.

Let it be and decline to roll on page 110
Roll the die on page 90
If you have the lucky die roll it on page 128

You clearly remember this path from your initial meeting with King Rolo long ago, and a wave of relief washes over you as you realize his private chambers are just down the hall. You've almost made it.

Unfortunately, this sense of ease is short-lived as you round the corner and freeze abruptly. There before you is a massive, growling dog, his eyes trained directly on you despite your attempt to use the shadows as cover.

The dog's snarls grow louder as he steps forward with horrifying menace. This canine is much larger than you expected, nearly filling the hallway with his muscular girth.

Try to calm and pet the guard dog on page 91
Run away to page 137
If you have the spaghetti, give it to the dog on page 216

You let the king's question linger in your mind for a while, rolling these options over in your head and considering which one of the bunch you connect with most. At first brush, all three of these paths seem like a tall order for a common peasant like yourself, but upon further consideration, one begins to shimmer and sparkle within your mind.

You find yourself pulling away, some inner voice refusing to accept the possibility of this heroic path.

There must be some kind of mistake, the inner voice insists.

You refuse to break, however, standing tall and proud. The more solid your visions of this potential future get, the more that inner voice of denial slowly fades away and disappears.

"I choose the wizard path," you announce proudly.

King Rolo nods, apparently pleased by this decision. "A fascinating pursuit," he offers. "I don't understand a word of it, but there's no question the power of magic can move kingdoms. You must know a little already, yes?"

"I've never done magic before," you admit.

The sentient twenty sided die's expression falters, but he makes his best attempt to stay optimistic. "Okay then, we'll start your training immediately. Exit my chambers and head to the left, go through the main foyer and beyond, into the East wing. There you'll find the wizard's tower. Grimble the Grey will be waiting for you."

You nod and take your leave, bowing to the king and exiting his chambers.

As you make your way through the castle, you can feel your anxiety growing, the seeds of self-doubt that lurk within you blossoming into horrible, destructive weeds. Is it really possible you hold the key to some ancient prophecy?

It's exciting in theory, but that's a lot of responsibility to heap on the shoulders of someone who feels, well, pretty average most of the time.

Eventually, you arrive at the wizard's tower, standing outside the chamber of Grimble the Grey. Not sure what else to do, you reach out and give the wooden double doors a firm knock.

"Hello?" you call. "I'm here to fulfill the prophecy?

There's a brief pause before the doors fly open to reveal a large bigfoot sporting grey robes and covered in similar fur.

"That sounded like more of a question than a statement," the wizard observes.

"I'm here to fulfill the prophecy," you repeat.

"Better," the bigfoot continues. "Come in."

You follow the enormous furry creature into his spell crafting laboratory, a dome-ceilinged stone room covered in ancient tomes and various arcane ingredients.

The bigfoot begins to circle, looking you over skeptically. He seems quite unconvinced by your presence, but in the spirit of due diligence he waves his hand in the air.

"Let's see what kind of aura we have here," the grey wizard continues.

A green glow suddenly erupts from your body, causing the bigfoot to jump back in alarm. He stumbles a bit, nearly toppling a nearby table of tinctures and scrolls before regaining his composure.

"Oh my god," Grimble offers in amazement, the words tumbling forth as he takes you in with wonder and awe. "The great role-player!"

By the time your aura fades his attitude has changed completely.

"You really *are* the one," Grimble the Grey says with a solemn nod. The bigfoot hurries over to his bookshelf and pulls out a thick, ancient tome.

Grimble approaches you with this massive book and drops it on the table before you with a loud thud. He opens it up, flipping through the old yellowing pages until finally arriving at the section he's looking for.

An image of another wizard's tower has been sketched upon the parchment below you, this building a dark and twisted reflection of the spire you currently stand in. There's something about its architecture that's undeniably wicked.

"An evil sorcerer at the edge of our world has discovered a new source of arcane power," Grimble explains. "His name is Count Storb. No longer content with the necromantic energy of life and death, he has harnessed the eternal cosmic emptiness of The Void itself."

"The black ooze," you reply with a nod.

"Yes," Grimble confirms. "This substance is bad enough on its own, but when combined with the creatures of our land, it has created all kinds of monstruous abominations. The fearsome beasts of our world are becoming more and more powerful, and soon enough the forces of good will no longer be able to push them back."

"How can we stop him?" you question.

"How can *you* stop him," Grimble corrects. "You are the one this prophecy speaks of, so the power is yours. It's up to you to travel to the dark wizard's tower and slay him dead."

"Oh," you stammer, suddenly feeling awkward about the task at hand. "Like... kill him?"

Grimble senses your hesitation. "I mean... if that's a problem for you, ethically speaking, you could just turn him into a frog."

You consider your mission a moment, still not entirely convinced this is the right path. It sounds quite thrilling, that's for sure, but dispatching an evil wizard is a lot to ask.

Accept your mission on page 189
Decline on page 69

Instead of throwing yourself into a needless battle, you decide to wait this one out. With the element of surprise in your favor, you're thoroughly convinced these sentient corn on the cob's wouldn't pose much of a problem, but does this world really need more bloodshed?

These bandits can't wait here all day.

You stay hidden in the bushes, watching the strange creatures from afar until, eventually, they pack up their things and move along.

When the coast is clear, you continue on your way.

Resume your journey on page 17

"It's your mother!" you cry. "They were attacked by a band of ruthless coblins and now they're clinging to life. Go! Be with your family in this time of need!"

The stegosaurus nods profusely, her panic growing. "But what of the castle? It's my duty to guard!"

"I've been assigned to your post," you continue. "Now go!"

The dinosaur turns to leave and you immediately relax, thankful your little story has managed to carry you this far. So much of the plan is riding on this moment, and you're thrilled to discover that it actually worked.

You watch as the guard disappears down the road, swallowed by the night.

The second the coast is clear you spring into action, slipping back through the gate and hurrying to the front doors of the castle.

Creep inside to page 89

"Wait!" you cry out. "Stop!"

Your friend slows down and turns back around, clearly frustrated but willing to listen to whatever's on your mind.

"You're very strong," you admit. "One of the most powerful creatures I've ever seen, to be honest, but you can't let that power rot away your soul. The Void is what we're fighting here, and using your magical gifts for rampant destruction is exactly what The Void wants."

Amanda is clearly upset by your words, fuming a bit as she listens. "You're just jealous!" the bumblebeeholder protests. "You hate that I'm better at magic so you're trying to keep me from using it!"

"That's not it at all," you reply, shaking your head profusely.

Attack her on page 130
If you have the 'turn into frog' scroll, use it to stop Amanda on page 26
Join her and destroy the town on page 107

62

While there's certainly something exciting about the world of sorcery and spell craft, you can't help the nagging feeling in the back of your mind that you just don't belong.

"I'm sorry," you offer the bigfoot. "I don't think this is for me."

Melovan is clearly disappointed, but he accepts with a solemn nod. Fortunately, your magical display has provided more than enough excited customers, and soon the bigfoot is back behind his stand, diligently working away as he exchanges gold coin for an assortment of magical wands.

You continue on your way, strolling through the market and taking in even more of the exciting sights and sounds. You don't get very far.

After a few steps you catch a sharp hiss from between two empty stalls, the abrupt noise halting you in your tracks and drawing your attention.

"Hey!" a figure offers, peaking around the corner and revealing themselves to be a light purple unicorn with a sparkling horn. They're clad in the soft leather outfit that's used by certified sneaks, a crew of outlaw thieves and rogues who live on the edge of society within Billings. "It's really you!"

"Me?" you question, a little confused.

The unicorn nods. "I saw you enter the market and followed you over here. What the hell are you doing?"

"I'm just... trying to find my way," you offer in return. "Do I know you?"

The unicorn shakes their head. "No, but *I* know you," he offers. "You're part of the prophecy. I'd recognize that face anywhere."

You let out an exhausted sigh. "I've been hearing this prophecy thing a lot today," you admit. "What makes you think your interpretation is the real one?"

"Because it's the prophecy they don't want you to know about," the unicorn sneak counters. "Come on, follow me."

With that, the unicorn ducks back behind an empty booth.

Go with the unicorn to page 48
Decline on page 28

You decide to adjust your aim the slightest bit to the left, recognizing that your throws usually have a hook to them. You envision the path of the rock in your hand, picture the way it will look and feel as it travels through the air in a clean, even arc and strikes your target.

You take a deep breath, then throw.

A loud, hollow thunk rings out through the empty back yard as your stone makes contact.

"Hell yeah!" you cry out, pumping your fist in the air then glancing at Lorbo in excitement.

Your friend isn't nearly as thrilled as you are, but he begrudgingly cracks a smile. "Alright, fine," he offers. "A deal's a deal."

Suddenly, the door opens behind you and Jorlin steps onto the porch. "Ready to talk?" he questions.

Lorbo laughs. "If you're ready to apologize."

"I mean... not really," Jorlin counters.

You interject quickly, hoping to head off this conversation at the pass. "Hey! Can't we just find a middle ground here?"

Lorbo takes a deep breath and lets it out, trying his best to be mature about this and to keep your wager in mind as he moves forward.

"Alright," Lorbo finally offers. "I'm sorry I get so caught up in the rules. I know it can be a little much sometimes, but without strict guidelines it's hard for me to care about what happens to our characters. There needs to be some *actual* danger, otherwise I don't have fun."

"But it's *fun* to let loose!" Jorlin counters. "Bad Boys and Buckaroos is all about letting your imagination fly."

"Not to everyone," Lorbo explains. "I enjoy that stuff, too, but having structure is really important to me. There's something in this game for everyone, and finding a balance is the only way to keep our group together."

A grin creeps its way across your face as you hear this, genuinely touched by the way your friends have managed to patch up their differences.

Jorlin nods along, listening intently and letting the words sink in. "Yeah, I'm sorry, too," he finally says. "You're right, there's no *correct* way to enjoy this game. We've gotta find a middle ground."

The three of us continue to talk and hash things out for a while, any animosity gradually slipping away as it's replaced by the pleasant warmth of friendship. It's easy to get carried away in the moment, but little conflicts like this are rarely worth self-destructing over. The thing that makes our gaming group so special isn't that we're all the same, it's that everyone's different. We all come at role-playing in our own way, and this cocktail of influences creates something really special.

Eventually, Sarah pokes her head outside. "You guys ready to get started again?" she questions.

Soon enough, the whole gang is hustling downstairs and returning to our seats around the wooden table. We settle in, gathering our dice and adjusting the papers in front of us.

Sarah clears her throat and turns directly toward you. "Alright, you were just meditating in a forest," she begins, describing the scene. "Your timeline split apart and you were falling through several layers of meta reality. Eventually, you arrived in this world, but you've managed to bring yourself back. Leaves rustle quietly as the afternoon breeze floats through them."

As your friend continues to describe the scene, you can feel yourself slipping deeper and deeper into your own body. The room around you is grows dimmer, until eventually you're surrounded by nothing but utter darkness.

Gradually, however, a faint light begins to appear. You can hear the chirping of birds and smell the sweet piney freshness of a deep forest.

You realize now that your eyes are closed, and the illumination you'd been sensing is the sun as it dances across the back of your eyelids.

You open your eyes.

"Welcome back, buckaroo," Chuck Tingle offers, the robed figure standing before you in the middle of the clearing.

You're perched atop the same stone platform from which you left, sitting cross-legged for who knows how long. You'd be just as surprised if someone revealed your meditation lasted three seconds or three days.

"That was... unexpected," you offer.

Chuck nods. "The path of the true buckaroo can be very unique, but then again all trots are."

"Did it work?" you suddenly blurt, deeply concerned about the outcome of your journey. "Is The Void gone?"

"The Void is nothingness," Chuck explains. "Your dang game was close to ending, so that nothingness was creepin' through the cracks like a devil in disguise. Got pretty heckin' close to consuming everything, but through your brave trot you managed to push it back and return light to this timeline! You fought the dang Void and you won, buckaroo!"

You erupt to your feet with excitement. "Really?" you cry out.

Chuck nods, then slowly backs away into the forest. "Don't worry, buckaroo. There's plenty more adventures to be had without the sick Void around, like finding a misplacer beast's forgotten keys or helping a dragon learn to kiss. You're gonna have so much fun with your buds."

Soon enough, the mysterious true buckaroo has disappeared into the wilds, leaving you completely alone. Moments later, however, another cascade of rustling leaves and murmuring voices begins to fill your ears.

"Who's there?" you call out.

Suddenly, Sarah, Lorbo and Jorlin emerge from the bushes, smiling wide as they greet you warmly. The four of you come together in an enormous hug, thrilled the adventuring party has come together. Your friends are clad in an assortment of vivid costuming, a wizard's robe for Sarah, a thieves utility suit for Lorbo, and a set of warrior's armor for Jorlin.

"Alright, what's next?" you finally ask as your embrace breaks, considering your options.

"Let's go find some adventure," Sarah replies. "Together."

You hoist your fist in the air as the other's raise their weapons and wands, cheering excitedly. Soon enough, you're heading off into the woods, no idea what could be lurking around the bend.

You're just excited to take it on with your friends.

THE END

You hold your breath, waiting for the bigfoot's back to turn. The second you see your opening, you reach up and snatch this delicious plate of SPAGHETTI off the counter before you. The movement is quick and silent, a perfect example of the training you've been so diligently working through over the last several weeks.

All of that preparation has come down to this tiny sleight of hand performance, and in the blink of an eye it's paid off.

Not wasting any time, you slink away from the kitchen and return to the castle's main foyer. Here, you begin to creep your way up the large staircase in utter silence. You're like a ghost, a phantom in the night who will avoid even the most scrutinizing efforts at detection.

Once reaching the upper level, you being to make your way down a series of long, twisting hallways.

Sneak along to page 55

You immediately turn and run down the hallway, readying your dungeon key as you approach the iron door that leads even deeper into this labyrinth. If you can slip inside quick enough, you just might lose your pursuers in the crumbling depths of the old dungeon.

Footsteps pound the stone floor behind you as you slip your key inside and twist hard, springing the lock and pulling hard to reveal another long set of stairs.

Before you get the chance to go any farther, however, you feel a sharp pain in your stomach. You glance down to discover a massive sword has been thrust clean through your body, glistening crimson in the flickering torchlight as it holds you in place.

You try to say something, but your voice spills out in an unintelligible gurgle of blood and spit.

"We've got the traitor," someone calls from behind you. "Looks like that prophecy wasn't everything it was cracked up to be."

You feel a large metal boot on your back as one of the guards braces himself against you, withdrawing his sword while simultaneously kicking you forward. Your strength decimated, you tumble off the edge of this long stone staircase, rolling end over end as you crash into the depths.

By the time you reach the bottom you're barely conscious, staring up at a sliver of light that grows thinner and thinner. The iron door slams shut with a clang as the darkness overwhelms you.

THE END

"Bad Boys and Buckaroos!" you offer, feeling a faint surge of inspiration deep inside of your belly.

Zippy opens one of the books and begins to look through it, marveling at all of the fantastical imagery.

"Do you play it on your computer?" he questions.

"Nope," you reply, shaking your head. "Just a pencil and some paper."

Zippy scrunches up his face in disgust when he hears this, but he doesn't put the book down. In fact, he seems even more fascinated than before.

"Can we play?" he finally questions.

Say "sure" on page 118
Say "maybe later" on page 150

"I'm sorry," you finally say, shaking your head from side to side. "I... can't."

"You *what?*" the wizard blurts, utterly dumbfounded.

"I want to help with your mission, but it feels a little too... violent. I may be part of some mysterious prophecy to save the world, but I don't think this is the right way to do it," you explain.

The bigfoot shakes his head from side to side, then lets out a long, defeated breath. "Alright then," is all he can think to say. "The prophecy still needs to be fulfilled, though."

"But how?" you question. "People keep trying to send me on these missions to save the world, but none of them seem like the right way to go about it. There's gotta be more to this than killing evil wizards. Why does the prophecy need to involve some great outward journey? What if the *real* key is looking inward?"

As you run though this with Grimble the Grey he becomes progressively more disappointed, eventually giving up completely.

"It sounds like the real path you're looking for is the way of the *true buckaroo,*" he finally admits.

"Really?" you reply, curiously. "Where do I start?"

"Head out past the city wall, into the fields and the woods beyond," the bigfoot explains. "There's a true buckaroo temple that will hold the answers you seek."

"Thank you," you reply, then turn and head back down the winding tower staircase.

Follow your heart to page 42
Follow your heart to page 42

"I'm sorry," you offer, then continue onward.

The die barely reacts, just slinking back into the shadows from which he came.

Soon enough, you find yourself creeping even deeper into this oppressive stone labyrinth. The upper levels of the dungeon were unpleasant enough, but with every step you grow even more uncomfortable. The air down here is cold and still, dank with the scent of rot and mold and death. The torches that illuminate your way have grown few and far between, and eventually you realize these flaming sconces were not lit by any official representatives of the kingdom. These are here for the troll.

You ready your dagger, slowing down a bit as you creep through the dim light of this underground layer.

Suddenly, movement.

You jump in alarm, ready to slash any monster who might charge out from the darkness, but what you encounter is much less threatening. Instead of an enormous troll coming to devour you whole, you find a small brown rat scurrying along the stone floor.

Something is tied to the creature's back, and you manage to snatch it up in your hands. The rodent immediately begins to squeal, attempting to bite you with its sharp little teeth, but before it has a chance you've already procured the item. You drop the rodent and watch as it scurries away, then look down to discover a rolled up parchment held tight within your grip.

You unfurl the scroll and read a sloppily written message within. "You are stupid, haha," you read aloud, utterly confused by this bizarre and aggressive message.

You notice a few more rats with notes tied to their backs as you continue onward, but these particular creatures are much too fast to catch.

Now the only thing more unpleasant than the ice cold air is the putrid scent that wafts through it. This odor that permeates everything has only grown throughout your journey, and as you arrive at the edge of a larger chamber it reaches its peak.

Eyes watering, you peek around the corner to find this room absolutely covered in trash. There are food wrappers everywhere, filth piled up to the ceiling as more rodents scurry about. In the corner is a scarecrow doll made up to resemble a fair maiden, with straw for hair and buttons for eyes.

Sitting in the middle of it all is a large green troll.

"What are you doing down here!" he snarls. "Leave my chambers at once!"

"I think it's time for you to move out," you counter.

"Make me," the troll snaps, then continues to ignore your presence.

You watch as the massive green beast picks up a rat from his trash pile, attaching a note to its back with some string and then sending it to scurry away.

"What's with the notes?" you question.

The troll frowns. "I like to send nasty anonymous messages around the kingdom. It's so *funny!*"

"I mean... it's not really that funny," you counter. "I guarantee you, this life of crafting rude messages in the darkness is much sadder than the situation of anyone who receives them."

"So?" the troll blurts, clearly not sure how to respond. "Who cares?"

You let out a long, frustrated sigh. "Listen, you just need to leave."

The troll shakes his head. "No way."

"Then I'll be forced to *make* you leave," you continue.

It's only now the troll catches sight of your dagger, realizing that you mean business.

"Tell you what," the creature gurgles. "I'll leave if you can beat me in an arm wrestling contest."

If you'd rather fight him turn to page 98
Agree to arm wrestle on page 178

You raise your staff and spring into action, rushing into the fray with your crackling blue weapon and tearing into these undead character sheets.

One of the zombies lurches toward you from the right, slow and steady as their mouth hangs open and a deep groan spills forth. You swing your staff like a bat, walloping them so hard they erupt in a sparkling explosion of blue energy.

Two more approach from the left, and you quickly dispatch them with a similar treatment. This time, however, the energy in your staff is weakened slightly. It takes two strikes to fell your opponents instead of a single powerful blow.

The character sheet zombies continue to pile on, and you gradually begin to realize there's simply too many of them to gain the upper hand. You find yourself backing away from the fray, pushed from a position of triumphant offense to panicked defense.

You're backing up now, swinging frantically as you struggle to keep the horde at bay. You manage to knock a few of the zombies down, but others just fall into line to take their place. Before long, there's just too many of the torn pages to manage.

The zombies overwhelm you, tearing you apart as you scream in agony.

THE END

"I think I'll stay here," you reply confidently.

The unicorn just stares at you for a moment, slightly confused. "Wait, what?"

"I'll take my chances," you offer, then hesitate. "Did I win? Was this another test?"

Before the sneak has a chance to respond you hear the dungeon door open with a loud clang and a cascade of footsteps rumbling down the nearby stairs. The unicorn immediately pulls back, disappearing into the shadows from which they came.

The next thing you know, a velociraptor guard is standing before you.

"Time to meet your maker, traitor," the dinosaur offers, pulling out his key and unlocking your cell.

"Wait!" you cry. "I was hoping we could talk about this!"

The second your cage is open two hulking royal guards enter, grabbing you roughly by each arm and dragging you out of your cell. You struggle to get away, but they're much too strong.

Soon enough, you're being carried up and out of the dungeon, the dinosaur captors leading your way as you traverse a long stone hallway. Up ahead is the shining light of day, and it's a great relief to see this symbol of warmth.

Unfortunately, any good will is crushed the second you emerge into a large town square.

A crowd has gathered, chattering excitedly as they part to reveal a massive gallows that awaits your arrival.

THE END

You head out to the back porch, pushing through the doorway slowly and then taking a seat next to Lorbo as he gazes out into the dark backyard. It's a pleasantly cool night, and for a moment it's nice to just sit here and let the sound of chirping crickets and croaking frogs soothe your senses.

Lorbo sips from his tall glass of chocolate milk, but he says nothing. He's deeply focused, his anger manifesting in a ferocious internal dialog that never quite boils high enough to reveal itself through the calm surface exterior. Eventually, he starts leaning down and picking up pebbles from the gravel path before you, tossing them across the yard and listening as they slip through bushes and leaves on the other side.

"I'm sick of Jorlin not giving a damn about the rules," Lorbo finally blurts, the first to speak. "The whole game falls apart if there's nothing concrete to pin it on."

To say "Jorlin is being a jerk." turn to page 115
To convince Lorbo it's all about finding a balance turn to page 215

Fortunately, as you slash away at this ferocious beast the sword in your hand grows with power. The magical energy that courses through your sizzling blade begins to arc and leap, dancing across your weapon in a visual manifestation of your mighty power as a warrior. All of your training has come down to this.

With one final slice, you break through the dragon's armored scales and split his belly down the middle. The monster lets out a deafening screech that rumbles through the cavern as its innards spill forth in a cascade of noxious black tar.

The Voidal infection had consumed everything within this beast.

Now, however, the bubbling black ooze has nowhere to go. It spills out and pools around the dragon, but in this moment its toxic connection has been severed. Color begins to seep into the dragon's scales once again, saturating from black, to grey, to bright pink.

On the trek back to Billings you notice the natural world shares a similar, brilliant alteration, colors appearing slightly more vibrant as The Void loses its grip. This horrific cosmic influence is not gone completely, but with the dragon slain you're off to a pretty good start.

The kingdom of Billings celebrates your return, citizens dancing in the street and a parade thrown in your honor. The city now has more chocolate milk than it knows what to do with, and it's not long before this sweet brown treat becomes the official beverage of Billings.

Lady Norbalo couldn't be prouder of the warrior you've become, but your training quickly ends. You're martial skills have grown well past any of her lessons, and the only choice now is to take up another mantel. It's time for *you* to become the teacher, opening up your own warrior training academy.

Now, the next generation of adventurers can rise up and take on The Void for themselves.

THE END

As your journey stretches onward you look back on this encounter with a misplacer beast as an important milestone, the point at which your training *really* began. There's only so much you can learn within the safety of the kingdom walls, and once you've ventured into the wilderness there are no second chances. You learned a lot from that battle, and the ones that followed shape you even more.

While the mission of taking on a mighty Voidal dragon had once seemed an impossibly daunting task, you find yourself growing stronger every day. You begin to feel a connection to your weapon that's almost mystical, a level of control very few warriors can hope to attain.

As ridiculous as the prophecy once seemed, you're now beginning to realize that your place as a true hero is not that far-fetched, and while this trust in yourself grows with every step, you're also aware the power was always lurking within you.

You just didn't know where to look.

At long last, you reach the base of the mountains. Much like your path as a warrior, gazing up from the bottom is a daunting sight, it's only when you start trudging along that you realize how mighty you actually are.

The air begins to thin, growing colder as you make your ascent. The tree covered landscape gradually falls away as snow and rocky crags replace their presence.

Still, you trudge onward, knowing somewhere atop this mountain lies the frightening dragon in his vast, cavernous lair.

You stop in your tracks as a thick spot of black ooze reveals itself before you in the stark white snow. This is your first evidence the dragon is nearby, prompting you to draw your weapon and take a defensive stance.

As you continue along, you notice more and more of these Voidal splatters, the collection gradually leading you to the mouth of a wide open cave. Peering inside, you see the whole place is illuminated by a beautiful phosphorescent fungi, lighting your way as you creep into its rocky depths.

Your ears are flooded with the sound of heavy breathing, the steady rumble of an absolutely massive creature at rest. With every step it grows louder, until eventually you round a corner to find the Voidal dragon itself, coiled atop a massive trove of chocolate milk bottles and deep in the arms of sleep.

The creature is gigantic and covered in scales that drip with a noxious black ooze, the bubbling tar pooling around him as he gurgles and heaves. A toxic mist swirls around the dragon's mouth, as though something terrible and corrosive lies hidden within his throat.

This is your chance, you suddenly realize, blown away by the luck that has somehow befallen you. With the dragon fast asleep, you should have no problem sneaking up and delivering an instant death blow.

Unfortunately, there's something about this approach that seems dishonorable, an offense to the warrior's code that has slowly become an important part of your life.

Wake the dragon and fight face to face on page 186
Sneak up and deliver a death blow on page 183

It takes a moment for the outright hostility of Lady Norbalo to finally sink in, but when it does it hits you like a truck. You've offered your services to fulfill this prophecy, but getting treated like trash along the way was never part of the deal. Yes, this unicorn is a great and powerful knight, but if they feel like your involvement in this quest is a waste of time then so be it.

"Deal with the troll yourself," you finally retort. "I quit."

You offer a smug grin and stroll past Lady Norbalo, making your way into the main foyer of the castle.

The unicorn calls after you, but she's too far away to hear now. Even if you could make out the words, you wouldn't be turning around.

Prophecies are open to interpretation, and this one is no different. Regardless, you're certain of one thing: that was not your path.

Out in the cobblestone streets of Billings, you march away from the castle with your head held high, happily welcoming the vast sea of options that spread out before you.

Eventually, however, a sobering realization washes through your mind. The role-playing session with your friends is over and done with, and now that you've decided against training with Lady Norbalo you've got no direction.

You take a deep breath and let it out, gathering your senses and struggling to find a path. If you are, in fact, part of a prophecy, then it's your duty to find the place where this journey *really* begins.

You glance to your left, your gaze falling upon a sprawling market bazaar full of unique characters, from peasants to the wealthy elite. They're all milling about as they shop for wares.

To the right is a very different path, a cobblestone road that leads all the way down to the city gates. Beyond are the wide open fields that surround Billings, golden grass shifting in the breeze on this peaceful afternoon.

One of these settings calls out to you, filling your heart with the promise of an adventure that's so much more than taking orders from an angry knight.

Head toward the city gate on page 220
Head toward the market on page 120

"Wait!" you cry out. "Stop!"

Your friend slows down and turns back around, clearly frustrated but willing to listen.

"I understand where you're coming from," you offer. "Having that much power is intoxicating, but it's worth *nothing* if you don't wield it with love in your heart."

"I *do* have love in my heart!" the bumblebeeholder protests. "I'd love to destroy that town!"

You shake your head solemnly. "That's not love," you continue. "I know you're riled up right now, but I think you'll agree with me if you just give it a little time. It's hard to encounter The Void and not take a little of that darkness with you."

Amanda shakes her head. "No way. Let's go."

You reach into your bag and pull out a delicious helping of honeysuckle candy, slowly unwrapping a piece. You had it over to your companion and then take one for yourself.

"Have some honeysuckle candy with me," you offer. "If you *still* want to destroy a town when we're done, then I'll be right there with you."

Of course, you're lying through your teeth, but you'll cross that bridge when you come to it.

Finally, Amanda agrees.

Soon enough, the two of you are sitting on a large boulder in the middle of the swamp, the bag of candy resting between you as you take down piece after piece of the delicious treat.   It tastes amazing.

The two of you start telling stories and cracking jokes, your laughter cascading across the marsh around you.

Eventually, however, you run out of candy.

"Alright, you ready to get going?" the bumblebeeholder asks.

You hesitate for a moment, then cautiously follow up with a very important question. "Back to Billings?"

Amanda looks confused. "Of course!"

Suddenly, she remembers the events that let up to your little dessert break. A mortified expression crosses the bumblebeeholder's face.

"I don't know what came over me," she finally offers, clearly ashamed.

You pat her on the shoulder. "The Void can be hard to shake sometimes," you offer. "It's okay. Just remember, love is the most powerful force of all."

Your friend nods and flutters up from the boulder, buzzing off into the swamp. "Let's go!" she calls back over her shoulder. "We've got a long walk ahead of us!"

You can't shake feeling this is the start of a beautiful friendship.

THE END

Thinking fast, you pull forth the web scroll from your bag and unfurl the parchment. You quickly scan over these arcane instructions, then center yourself and begin to read.

"Spideralis webendron!" you bellow, performing the magic incantation and directing all of your energy toward this mob of oncoming zombies.

Suddenly, a sticky webbing manifests itself across this undead character sheet horde, trapping them beneath its heavy weight like an otherworldly blanket. The zombies cry out, struggling to free themselves and finding very limited success.

Out of the whole horde, only one of the undead pages manages to free themselves. The zombie staggers about, still covered in stringy web, then tumbles into one of the hanging wall torches.

The results are immediate. There's a brilliant eruption of dancing light as the paper goes up in flames, shrieking wildly as its erratic movements become even more chaotic. This web covered ignition source then tumbles into the rest of the character sheets, causing them to ignite with the same velocity.

Soon enough, the whole tower is burning, the walls and ceiling rolling with sheets of orange as the heat washes over you.

It's through this terrifying landscape that the dark sorcerer appears before you, a stegosaurus in a long black cloak at the top of the staircase.

"The prophecy is a fool's errand," the dinosaur bellows. "My magic is too powerful to succumb to the promises of some ancient wishful thinking. This world belongs to The Void now."

If you have the 'turn into frog' scroll, use it on page 124
Retreat to page 140
If you have the blue staff, attack on page 97
If you have the orange staff, attack on page 135

Typically, your morning wakeup call is the local rooster who perches atop a nearby cottage and crows gleefully at the rising sun. It's a routine you've grown to enjoy, a consistent start to your day, but this particular morning your wakeup call is truly spectacular.

Just a few minutes before the rooster has a chance to crow, another distinct sound echoes through the kingdom of Billings, and it's this cacophony that pulls you from your slumber with a smile already plastered across your face.

You sit up in bed, listening closely as the excited cries of a single citizen are joined by another, and another. Soon enough, people are erupting out of their homes in anger over all that racket, then swiftly yanked into a state of overwhelming joy and celebration.

You climb out of bed, pulling on your clothes and strolling through your small cottage to the front door.

Setting outside, you find the cobblestone streets are flooded with peasants, some of them hugging excitedly while others literally dance in the streets. Some just wear expressions of bemused confusion across their faces.

Upon every doorstep is a small bag, each one filled with an equal share of King Rolo's treasure horde courtesy of the Billings' sneak's guild.

You have to admit, you were prepared for the worst when it came to this final step of your plan, well aware people might begin snatching up the bags of their neighbors before anyone had a chance to discover their gift.

Amazingly, this doesn't happen, and while things are certainly wild and chaotic, there's a powerful haze of unbridled joy that works its way through everything.

"Wait! Wait!" comes a furious voice, these cries bellowing out through the city streets.

You glance up to see King Rolo hovering down the lane, flanked by two royal guards as he desperately tries to gather up his treasure.

"Who did this?" screams the king in a belligerent rage. "Tell me who is responsible and I will take their head!"

King Rolo focuses his attention on a young boy, grabbing him by the collar and causing the child to drop his bag of gold to the ground in fear.

"If I do not get an answer, then I will execute every child in this kingdom," the sentient die announces. "Starting with this one!"

If you have the 'turn into frog' scroll turn to page 111
If you don't have the 'turn into frog' scroll turn to page 148

"I used to play this game called Bad Boys and Buckaroos," you finally admit. "I was just thinking about all the fun times we had. My group had a falling out years ago."

Ashley's eyes go wide. "Wait, seriously?" she blurts. "I've always wanted to try playing Bad Boys and Buckaroos!"

Her reaction is even better than you'd imagined, and you can't help but feel that old spark of role-playing excitement ignite somewhere deep within.

"Could you come by my place and run a game?" Ashley continues.

You nod. "I know how to Tingle Master," you reply, the floodgates of your excitement opening even wider. "We've just gotta find one more player. Two is fine, I suppose, but a group works best."

Ashley smiles and nods. "Alright then. See who you can find and let's talk at the end of the day."

Your friend leaves you to it, going about her business once more as you sit lost in thought. There are several folks around the office who would make great additions to the game, but you've gotta choose carefully. Not everyone's reaction is gonna be as great as Ashley's.

Some folks will say they want to play, but when it comes time to sit down around the table and dive in, they become stiff, awkward or insincere at worst. You need to find another player who's going to be committed to a game.

That can be difficult to find.

Suddenly, your mind is flooded with visions of Lorbo and Jorlin, recalling the big fight that put an end to your last adventure. You can't let that happen again.

Focusing up, you start considering your other coworkers. There are three people you could potentially ask to join.

Gorb is a hard working intern, young and excited. He's a little flighty and tough to pin down, but once he's invested in a project he does a hell of a job.

Krimble is your boss at the top of the food chain. He's a bit rough around the edges, and certainly a dangerous ask, but if he joins the game then scheduling would be a lot easier. You're constantly surprised by his interests, and Bad Boys and Buckaroos could very well be right up his alley.

Last is Limber, a shy woman who doesn't talk much but has special rapport with you. She's still pretty quiet, but in the few times you've interacted, you've learned that she's exceptionally kind. Folks who are too self-conscious to participate can make things tough in a Bad Boys and Buckaroos group, but at the end of the day there's nothing better than a wholesome player who wants everyone to have a good time.

To ask Gorb turn to page 132
To ask Krimble turn to page 184
To ask Limber turn to page 160

86

Seeing your chance you decide to go for the dragon's heart, rushing toward the creature and courageously swinging away. Your weapon ricochets off the armored scales again and again, but still you push onward, struggling to produce any effect upon this massive beast.

The dragon, however, remains unphased. Soon enough, the monster has regained its bearings, and although one eye is oozing forth even more dark liquid than before, it's still perfectly capable of using the other.

Now that you're well within range, the monster reaches down and scoops you up in one of his razor sharp claws. You struggle to free yourself, lashing about in an attempt to slip through its scaly fingers, but your attempts are as fruitless as your attacks on the dragon's heart.

The creature holds you up in front of his mouth then belches forth a tidal wave of sticky black tar, the toxic mess washing over you and covering your body. You open wide to scream but the ooze quickly fills you up, wrapping you in its cold embrace.

The next thing you know, the dragon's claws are no longer squeezed tight around you. You are free, but floating in an infinite abyss of cosmic emptiness.

You make a brief attempt to swim to the surface, but you quickly realize there's no surface to be found. Endless nothingness lies in every direction, a plane of all that cannot be.

The very thought of this pushes you into a state of utter madness, your mind struggling to understand what's happening to the world around you as existence itself collapses like the center of a dying black hole.

The Void consumes you.

THE END

The wilds can be an unsettling place, that's for sure, and the last thing you want to do is overreact. There's plenty of traveling ahead, and if you stop and hide every time you get a strange feeling out here in the forest, then you'll never get anywhere.

Instead, you plow onward, your head held high as you focus on the task at hand: reaching the dark tower.

Unfortunately, this appears to be one of those cases where hiding was probably a better idea.

You travel twenty yards or so before a group of coblins springs out of the thick underbrush on either side, causing a startled yelp to escape your throat.

Coblins are short, sentient corn on the cob's, a ruthless species of living object who patrol these areas as small war bands. They are carnivores, and enjoy the taste of human flesh on occasion. Thankfully, most of these roadside assaults are strictly for profit, small time bandit raids where they steal your items and take off into the forest.

This particular group of coblin bandits are well armed, equipped with spears and clubs which they raise menacingly.

The lead coblin steps forward from the pack. "Wizard! Robes!" she shouts.

You nod along. "Yes, I'm a wizard."

"Magic items!" the leader shouts. "Now!"

"You want me to give you my magic items?" you scoff.

Sensing the rude tone of your voice, the sentient corns respond in turn. They push closer, their spears thrusting angrily in your direction while they amplify their threatening posture.

"Now!" the lead coblin screams again.

To claim you have no items turn to page 131
To hand over your scrolls and claim it's all you have turn to page 7
Attack with your staff on page 168
If you have a web scroll and want to use it turn to page 50

You decide to go for the dragon's heart, rushing toward the creature and courageously swinging away. Your weapon ricochets back off the armored scales again and again, but still you push onward, struggling to produce any effect upon this massive beast.

The dragon, however, remains unphased.

Now that you're well within range, the monster reaches down and scoops you up in one of his razor sharp claws. You struggle to free yourself, lashing about in an attempt to slip through its scaly fingers, but your attempts are as fruitless as your attacks on the dragon's heart.

The creature holds you up in front of his mouth then belches forth a tidal wave of sticky black tar, the toxic mess washing over you and covering your body. You open wide to scream but the ooze quickly fills you up, wrapping you in its cold embrace.

The next thing you know, the dragon's claws are no longer squeezed tight around you. You are free, but floating in an infinite abyss of cosmic emptiness.

You make a brief attempt to swim to the surface, but you quickly realize there's no surface to be found. Endless nothingness lies in every direction, a plane of all that cannot be.

The very thought of this pushes you into a state of utter madness, your mind struggling to understand what's happening to the world around you as existence itself collapses like the center of a dying black hole.

The Void consumes you.

THE END

The main foyer of the castle opens up before you, a grand hall that's hustling and bustling by daytime but vacant by night. The last time you were here, you'd been summoned by King Rolo himself and greeted as an honored guest. Now you're an outsider, creeping through the dimly lit chamber in direct defiance of royal order.

The success of this mission depends on a series of very specific steps, a method of reaching King Rolo's private chambers that has been devised through weeks of careful planning and reconnaissance.

The first of these steps is simple enough. The castle is known for its guard dog, a large and loyal creature who patrols the upper corridors at night. This ferocious canine has taken care of his fair share of intruders, but you're fortunate enough to know the key to his heart.

When the pup isn't busy devouring thieves and other riff-raff who've managed to get inside, he's gobbling down huge plates of spaghetti from the castle kitchen. It is said the guard dog has an overwhelming appetite for this specific meal, prepared in a distinct way that only the royal chefs are capable of.

Now, all you need to do is sneak into the kitchen and find some spaghetti before making your way to the upper landing.

Using your sneak training, you creep deeper into this massive structure. By now, the staff should all be fast asleep, or at least turned in for the night, but to your disappointment you notice a faint light emanating from within the kitchen.

The light moves gently from one side of the room to the other, then back again, a lantern carried from place to place as someone goes about their business. It's likely there's been an after-hours request from the castle cook.

You're suddenly faced with a very important decision. Do you risk snatching some spaghetti while the kitchen is occupied, or do you head upstairs and take your chances with a guard dog that might be parked right outside King Rolo's chambers?

Steal the spaghetti on page 155
Leave the spaghetti on page 191

You accept the twenty sided die, rolling it gently in your hands to get a sense of the weight. This is a hell of a toss, and it's hard not to think about all the variations at play. Would it land on a twenty if you threw it right now? What if you waited another thirty seconds?

Of course, none of that really matters. There's no way to tell what lies right around the corner; you've just gotta take your shot when you can.

You find a perfectly flat headstone, then carefully make your roll. You watch as the die bounces and tumbles, finally coming to rest on the absolute last result you'd want to see.

"One," you read aloud.

Suddenly, an assortment of skeletal hands burst through the dirt around you, causing a startled scream to erupt from your throat. You immediately try pulling away, but their bony grip is too strong.

For every set of undead fingers you slip through, another grabs you and pulls you deeper into the shifting ground. You cry out again, but by now they've dragged you well below the surface. Your mouth fills with dirt as you disappear completely.

THE END

You do everything you can to soften your demeanor, lowering your voice to a whisper as you raise your hands in a non-threatening stance.

"I'm not going to hurt you," you coo. "I just wanna pet this good dog."

The canine's growling lowers in volume, a great sign, and he seems to relax a bit.

You slowly move your hand towards him.

"That's it," you continue. "You're a good boy."

Suddenly, the dog snaps its jaws forward in a powerful bite. You yank back your fingers and feel a rush of relief as they're extracted without effort. A narrow miss, you think to yourself, before abruptly realizing that you're entire hand is missing and a bloody stump sits in its place.

You let out a horrified scream, falling back as the guard dog lunges onto you. The creature begins to bite and shake with its enormous teeth, easily tearing through your flesh.

You spent all this time avoiding the guards, and suddenly you've found yourself begging they'd come sooner. By the time they arrive there's nothing left of you to save.

THE END

Drawn in by the muscular man's winning smile, you finally decide to go with Billings Big Bucks.

"That one," you offer, tapping on the glass.

Jorlin nods and the cashier reaches in to extract your chosen ticket, handing it over as Jorlin pays.

Soon enough, the two of you are strolling back to the house as your friend sips away at his cold chocolate milk. His mood is already starting to improve, and for a moment you consider just forgetting about the lottery card in an effort to ride this wave of good vibes.

Before you have a chance, however, your friend pulls out a coin and flashes you his ticket. "Let's see if tonight's our lucky night," he offers, finishing his milk and tossing it into a trash can. Jorlin approaches a nearby wall and presses his ticket against it, using the hard surface as he scratches away at the little cartoon treasure chests.

Slowly, various numbers are revealed, but the longer Jorlin spends scratching away at this tiny card, the more his mood begins to shift back toward anger and frustration.

Eventually, he reaches the last chest.

"Here goes nothing," Jorlin announces.

Your friend begins to scratch away. Gradually, a smile begins to creep its way across his face. "I won!" he suddenly blurts, his eyes transfixed on the ticket gripped tight within his fingers. "Holy shit! I won!"

"Are you kidding?" you reply, utterly shocked. "How much?"

"A dollar," Jorlin announces.

Your heart quickly returns to its normal rate, but any sense of disappointment never comes. Despite this small prize, the simple act of winning has changed Jorlin's mood entirely. There's a spring in his step, and as the two of you continue back toward Lorbo's house you find yourself growing cautiously optimistic about this whole situation.

"I think you're right," Jorlin says as you reach the front walk. "We *do* need to find a middle ground. I was being a dick."

You push into the house, then make your way down a hallway toward the back yard. Lorbo is waiting on the porch, sipping from a cold glass of chocolate milk.

"Hey," you offer as Jorlin and you step outside to join your friend. Your voice is cool and calm, and you hope to keep things that way.

"Ready to talk?" Jorlin questions.

Lorbo laughs. "If you're ready to apologize," he snaps.

So much for keeping things cool and calm.

"I mean... I was *considering* it," Jorlin counters. "Don't you understand it's fun to let loose sometimes? Bad Boys and Buckaroos is all about letting your imagination fly."

"Not to everyone," Lorbo explains. "I like that stuff, too, but having structure is really important to me. There's something in this game for everyone, and finding a balance is the only way to keep this group together."

Jorlin nods along, listening intently and letting these words sink in. "Yeah, I'm sorry, too," he finally says. "You're right, there's no right way to enjoy this game. We've gotta find a middle ground."

The three of us continue to talk and hash things out for a while, any animosity gradually slipping away as it's replaced by the pleasant warmth of friendship. It's easy to get carried away in the moment, but little conflicts like this are rarely worth self-destructing over. The thing that makes your gaming group so special isn't that you're all the same, it's that everyone's a little different. We all come at role-playing in our own way, and this cocktail of influences creates something really special.

Eventually, Sarah pokes her head outside. "You guys ready to get started again?" she questions.

Soon enough, the whole gang is hustling downstairs and returning to their seats around the wooden table. You settle in, gathering your dice and adjusting your papers.

Sarah clears her throat and turns directly toward you. "Alright, you were just meditating in the forest," she begins, describing the scene. "Your timeline split apart and you were falling through several layers of meta reality. Eventually, you arrived in this world, but you've managed to bring yourself back. Leaves rustle quietly as the afternoon breeze floats through them."

As your friend continues to describe the scene, you can feel yourself slipping deeper and deeper into your own body. The room around you grows dimmer, until eventually you're surrounded by nothing but utter darkness.

Gradually, however, a faint light begins to appear. You can hear the chirping of birds and smell the sweet piney freshness of a deep forest.

You realize now that your eyes are closed, and the light you'd been sensing is the sun as it dances across the back of your eyelids.

You open your eyes.

"Welcome back, buckaroo," Chuck Tingle offers, the robed figure standing before you in the middle of the clearing.

You're perched atop the same stone platform from which you left, sitting cross-legged for who knows how long. You'd be just as surprised if someone revealed your meditation lasted three seconds or three days.

"That was... unexpected," you offer.

Chuck nods. "The path of the true buckaroo can be very unique, but then again all trots are."

"Did it work?" you suddenly blurt, deeply concerned about the outcome of your journey. "Is The Void gone?"

"The Void is nothingness," Chuck explains. "Your dang game was close to ending, so that nothingness was creepin' through the cracks like a devil in disguise. Got pretty heckin' close to consuming everything, but through your brave trot you managed to push it back and return light to this timeline! You fought the dang Void and you won, buckaroo!"

You erupt to your feet with excitement. "Really?" you cry out.

Chuck nods, then slowly backs away into the forest. "Don't worry, buckaroo. There's plenty more adventures to be had without the sick Void around, like finding a misplacer beast's forgotten keys or helping a dragon learn to kiss. You're gonna have so much fun with your buds."

Soon enough, the mysterious true buckaroo has disappeared into the wilds, leaving you completely alone. Moments later, however, another cascade of rustling leaves and murmuring voices begins to fill your ears.

"Who's there?" you call out.

Suddenly, Sarah, Lorbo and Jorlin emerge from the bushes, smiling wide as they greet you warmly. The four of you come together in an enormous hug, thrilled the adventuring party has come together. Your friends are clad in an assortment of vivid costuming, a wizard's robe for Sarah, a thieves utility suit for Lorbo, and a set of warrior's armor for Jorlin.

"Alright, what's next?" you finally ask as your embrace breaks, considering your options.

"Let's go find some adventure," Sarah replies. "Together."

You hoist your fist in the air as the other's raise their weapons and wands, cheering excitedly. Soon enough, you're heading off into the woods, no idea what could be lurking around the bend.

You're just excited to take it on with your friends.

THE END

96

"Honestly," you finally reply. "I'm just pretty exhausted. That was a long quest, and I'd like to go home now."

The unicorn is clearly disappointed with this response, staring at you a moment longer and then finally stepping back into the shadows without a word.

As the fires die completely and this massive spire returns to its former glory, free from Voidal influence, you find the sneak's words lingering in your mind.

Who knows what the real prophecy is?

Truth be told, you're tired of running around from one problem to the next. Whether it's cleaning up messes for the king or creeping around on behalf of some underground thieves' collective, you've done your part.

As you gaze around this beautiful, sparking tower you suddenly realize it's found itself without a resident. The trek back to Billings is long, and it'll still be there if you ever want to return.

Right now, however, it's time to relax.

You decide to head upstairs and explore the rest of this glorious magical tower on the edge of the world. It's already starting to feel like home.

THE END

You raise your staff and charge toward Count Storb, facing your opponent head on as the fire rages around you.

The dinosaur moves to meet you halfway, raising his hands and blasting forth a bolt of crackling necromantic energy from his fingertips. You immediately raise your staff to block this surge of arcane power, and for the most part it works. Your staff receives the brunt of this power blast, consuming the lighting before it has a chance to affect you, but it quickly becomes apparent this will only work so many times.

You reach the dinosaur and swing your weapon, slamming into him as a brilliant flash of blue energy fills the room. Count Storb is pushed back by this monumental attack but he stays on his feet, sliding across the ground as he braces himself against this magical force.

The stegosaurus raises his hands and blasts forth another surge of dark magic, only amplified by its deep connection to the endless cosmic Void. Again, you raise your staff to defend yourself, but now your weapon has been significantly weakened. The might of this arcane bolt splinters your staff in an eruption of blue energy.

Now defenseless, you make one last attempt to rush Count Storb. The dinosaur grins, realizing he now has the upper hand.

The third and final blast erupts from Storb's fingertips, tearing through your body and stripping the flesh from your bones in a powerful wave of necrotic destruction. Seconds later, your entire being has turned to ash, crumbling to the floor and mixing with the remnants of this burning structure.

THE END

This creature is much too large to beat in an arm wrestling match, which leaves you a single, frightening option.

As you reach for your dagger the troll lunges toward you, trash spilling off his large body as he staggers forward and swipes with a long, clawed hand.

You duck, narrowly avoiding his sharp nails and then rushing toward the monster with your dagger ready. You stab with a sharp, quick movement, piecing the beast's green flesh with your blade and then pulling back to see a spurt of dark liquid trickle forth. Unfortunately, the wound isn't nearly as devastating as you'd hoped, the troll's tough leather hide proving quite difficult to puncture.

You go in for another stab, but the troll pushes you back with such force that the blade goes flying from your hands. There's a loud clatter as the *DAGGER* slides across the floor and down into an iron grate. Your weapon is gone.

You climb to your feet and quickly gather your bearings, circling this garbage covered chamber as you square off with your monstrous opponent. You dodge the troll's swiping claws, your gaze darting around the room in search of *anything* that might help pull you out of this mess.

The first thing you spot is a sharp bone that rests nearby, likely the remains of another adventurer who tried to confront this horrible troll. With your dagger long gone, this could make a great replacement.

The other interesting feature you notice is a large stone post on the right side of the chamber. It appears to be a load bearing column, and if you can somehow maneuver yourself correctly, you just might convince the troll to accidently strike this segment. If the beast swings hard enough, the whole ceiling might come collapsing down on top of him.

Orchestrate a chamber collapse on page 222
Go for the sharp bone on page 147

While the prospect of putting an end to this battle right here and now is quite tempting, there's something about the whimpering, frightened beast that gives you pause. You suddenly find yourself overwhelmed with sympathy.

The dragon and its Voidal influence are two completely different things, and there's gotta be a way to separate them.

"I don't wanna hurt you," you call out, causing the dragon to grunt loudly. "I know you're not trying to do bad things, but The Void's hold on you is strong."

The dragon just breathes in deep and lets it out, black tar bubbling from its nostrils as it lays in defeat.

"I'm not going to kill you," you continue.

To your amazement, the dragon's jet black scales are beginning to lighten, transitioning into a dull grey.

"I'm so sorry this happened," you continue.

Soon enough, a warm, pink saturation begins to flood across the dragon with glorious vibrancy.

Your heart slamming within your chest, you walk toward the creature and open your arms, wrapping them around the beast's massive head and offering a loving hug.

"I'm so sorry," the dragon suddenly gushes, "I don't know what came over me."

By now the Voidal influence has been completely drained, your reptilian friend showing his true colors in beautiful neon pink.

Back at the Billings castle, a shadow sweeps across the marketplace. The citizens glance up, confused at first and then utterly horrified. They scream in alarm.

A massive pink dragon is hovering overhead. People begin to scatter, but when the dragon refuses to attack them their frantic escapes slow to a halt. The peasants return their gazes skyward, realizing now that someone is riding on the back of this massive beast.

You wave down to them, smiling wide.

100

Held tight in the dragon's claws is a massive bundle of chocolate milk bottles, the whole trove wrapped in fabric.

You're here to share, and there's plenty to go around.

THE END

You pull out your 'turn into frog' scroll and begin to read, briskly sweeping through the incantation before the dark sorcerer before you has time to react.

A surge of green crackling rings has already started to bloom around you, growing in size and then launching out at your dinosaur attacker. The second Count Storb is struck by these rings he begins to shift and change, the body once capable of delicate and complex arcane movements appearing awkward and stilted. He begins to collapse as he runs, his legs disappearing beneath him, and before the sorcerer has a chance to hit the ground his frame has altered completely.

A small green frog now sits in the count's place, harmless and confused as the orange blaze continues to rise around you.

Thinking fast, you rush over and scoop up the tiny amphibian, tossing it into your bag and sprinting back to the front doors. Brick and wood cascades down around you, narrowly missing your head as throw yourself through the exit in a final escape.

You splash into the swamp outside as the whole building comes tumbling down behind you, collapsing in a plume of flame and ash.

Back in Billings a parade is thrown in your honor, and while your new room in the castle provides a spectacular view, you decide to go down and check out the festivities up close. This is *your* parade, after all, and the feast to follow will be something to remember.

With the prophecy fulfilled, The Voidal influence has slowy started dissipating across the land. Monsters are retreating into the wilds and peace is returning to the kingdom of Billings.

These days, it's hard to imagine the little captive frog on your desk causing so many problems.

You stroll over and check on his cage, making sure there's plenty of water to drink and grubs to eat.

"You gonna be okay in here while I check out the parade?" you ask the tiny amphibian.

The frog just stares at you, blinking a few times but otherwise unresponsive.

"I'll give you a nice view," you offer, picking up the cage and carrying it over to a windowsill. "There you go."

102

With that, you turn to head out and enjoy your day. You pull open the door of your chambers and stop abruptly to find Grimble the Grey waiting for you.

"I'm sorry, I didn't want to disturb," the wizard offers.

"It's no problem," you reply, greeting your bigfoot companion warmly.

"Are you excited for tonight's feast?" the wizard continues.

"Of course," you retort with a nod, gradually realizing this is much more than a casual visit. There's something on Grimble's mind.

The wizard clears his throat. "I remember when you first arrived in the wizard's tower," Grimble begins. "I didn't know what to think, and I must admit I doubted you at first. Now I know how wrong I was. The student has become the teacher."

You laugh. "I don't know if that's true, old friend," you offer.

"It is," Grimble insists. "With your permission, I'd like to announce you as a new member of the wizard's high council. In a few years, I'd like you to take my place so I can move on to other pursuits."

"Wait, what?" you blurt. "Really?"

The bigfoot nods. "It would be an honor to have you."

You consider his offer for a moment, hesitant to put yourself in a position of such high regard. Deep down, you still feel like you're an imposter here.

Grimble notices this hesitation, smirking playfully. "If you feel like you don't belong on the high council, there's a frog in your office that says otherwise. You deserve this."

You nod, finally accepting your place as a hero.

"Alright. I'm in," you reply.

THE END

While there's certainly a time and place for the power of love, you decide to draw on simmering anger and frustration to pump yourself up.

You focus this rage, then reach out and take the troll's hand in yours. The two of you stare at one another across the table, eyes locked as the countdown begins.

"Three, two, one," you say in unison.

Suddenly, the two of you are pushing hard against one another, your palms wobbling back and forth as you struggle to force the troll down. His size is a huge advantage, but your predictions about the creature's actual strength we're dead on.

Still, arm wrestling a troll is no easy task, and you feel your muscles quickly beginning to weaken. You're slipping, the strength draining out of your body as fatigue overwhelms you.

It's time to turn on the afterburners.

You close your eyes, allowing the anger to overwhelm you. Almost instantly, the energy within your hand alters course. You can feel your power growing, the tides of this battle shifting as you slowly push back against the troll.

But this last minute push is short lived. Suddenly, the troll concentrates all of his might and flips the momentum completely. The creature slams your hand against the table with a loud bang as searing pain erupts across your body.

"Oh my god!" you scream, looking down at your appendage with wide-eyes shock. "You broke my arm!"

To your horror, a sharp white bone has punctured through your own skin.

"I'll never be a warrior now!" you scream. "How can I save the kingdom if I've gotta wait for my arm to heal?"

The troll grins, displaying his enormous rows of razor sharp teeth for the first time. "You're right," he replies. "Looks like there's only one use for you now."

Before you have a chance to react, the creature grabs you with both of his enormous arms and snaps his head forward. The troll opens wide with his giant maw, closing down with a forceful bite and severing you at the waist.

104

In your last few seconds of awareness you feel your torso sliding down the massive creature's throat.

THE END

You rush over to the corpse of your fallen attacker, immediately getting to work as you search underneath the creature's heavy canine body. The dark fur of this misplacer beast is thick and unruly, easily capable of hiding your missing weapon, but as you sweep your hand under the monster's fallen form you continue coming up short.

You even go so far as you sweep your hand through the beast's innards, wondering if you'd stabbed too deep and accidently lost track of your blade in the depths of its hungry stomach. Still, there's no sword to be found.

The howls of the approaching pack grow louder and louder, filling you with dread. You're just about to turn and run when a final, last minute idea suddenly crosses your mind.

Misplacer beasts typically manifest lost items in the last place you'd ever look, and with this in mind you reach behind the fallen canine's ear.

Suddenly, you gasp, wrapping your hand around your weapon's hilt and pulling it forth.

You'd love to stay and celebrate, but with no time to spare you immediately take off into the grass, running as fast as you can with your head ducked below the surface of this endless yellow field.

Your breathing heavy, you focus on working your arms and legs to push you deeper and deeper into the golden expanse. When you just can't take it anymore you collapse to the ground, struggling to stay quiet despite your heavy breathing.

You make yourself as small as possible, then wait.

Gradually, the seconds become minutes, time stretching on and on and the pack of ferocious beasts nowhere to be found. You realize slowly that, through some strange twist of fate, you've managed to escape the creatures with your sword in tow.

Your quest continues on page 76

106

You quietly unfurl the web scroll in your bag, looking over the instructions for this powerful incantation as you creep toward the living vegetables. You take note of where each of them is, careful to focus your magical energy in such a way that every single coblin will be fully trapped within this sticky arcane substance.

Finally, you loudly bellow the magic words. *"Spideralis webendron!"*

The second this incantation leaves your lips a brilliant flash erupts from the *WEB SCROLL*. The document immediately turns to dust, falling through your fingers in a fine grey mist, but the manifestation that lies before you is much more impressive.

Every single coblin has found themselves caught in a sticky web, much like that of a spider only hundreds of times larger. They are absolutely covered in this thick substance, held in place and shrieking in frustration and confusion.

"Crime doesn't pay!" you proudly announce to the howling corn on the cob bandits, feeling like a total bad ass. "I'm sure some of the rangers patrolling these woods will find you and clean up this mess. They might throw you in jail, but they also might just pop you over a fire. Either way, I'm not sticking around to find out."

You creep over the scattered webs and the coblins trapped within, continuing on your way.

Resume your journey on page 17

Maybe it's the fact that you're terrified by the power your friend so flagrantly wields, or maybe there's a spark of darkness lurking deep inside you and its finally been given the fuel to ignite. Either way, your demeanor suddenly makes a monumental shift.

"Okay then" you reply. "Let's destroy the town."

Amanda's eyes flash with excitement. "Really?"

"Sure," you offer. "Why not?"

The two of you begin trekking through the swamp, and with every step toward your destination you can feel something growing inside you. There's a dark space deep within the pit of your stomach, a patch that's not warm, nor cold; an endless abyss.

By the time you recognize this as The Void itself, it's already too late to alter course. You've committed to this path, and there's no turning back now.scri

Gradually, the edge of this little hamlet comes into view as the swamp transitions into a thick green forest. You can see they've built a modest wall around the city, a handful of guards patrolling the top.

The guards wave as you approach, no reason to see you and your friend as any sort of threat until, suddenly, Amanda tears through four of them with a bolt of magical energy.

Soon enough, the townsfolk are screaming in horror, running this way and that as you and your companion get to work vaporizing them with a cascade of magical abilities.

The Void has fully consumed you, easily transferring from Count Storb to its new host.

You relish this destruction, the pleasure that you once found in personal fulfillment now warping into some macabre parody of itself. At one point, you actually start laughing.

Suddenly, however, you feel a sharp pain in your chest. You glance down to see an arrow has been fired into your heart, the shaft sticking straight out of you as a small pool of blood seeps through the fabric of your clothes.

You glance up to see a band of three heroes standing proudly; a wizard, a warrior, and a true buckaroo.

"Amanda!" you cry out, looking for help.

The bumblebeeholder is quick to come to your aid, but before she has a chance to fire off another bolt of yellow energy, a sneak emerges from the shadows and stabs her in the back with a tiny, poison soaked dagger.

"Hey! What the hell?" the bumblebeeholder gasps, swaying in the air for a moment and then slamming into the ground with a loud thud.

The sneak hurries back and rejoins his friends, an evenly balanced four-person adventuring party.

"You should've stayed a hero," their warrior leader calls out.

You stagger a moment longer then collapse into the dirt next to Amanda, the two of you taking your place as defeated villains.

THE END

You dive to the left, but the misplacer beast skillfully predicted your move and lands directly on top of you.

The creature is an enormous canine with jet black fur and sharp, gnashing teeth. It stands on four muscular legs and is approximately eight feet long, but the thing that's truly frightening about this ferocious creature are the two tentacles that rise from either shoulder blade. These slithering appendages are incredibly powerful, used to slash and whip their prey, and feature spiked pads at the end of their fur-covered length.

Of course, this fearsome predator is more than just its physical presence. All misplacer beasts are humming with magical energy, an unseen force that constantly swirls around them and causes their opponents to misplace things.

Right now, however, the only thing you really care about are the monster's enormous jaws as they ravenously snap just inches away from your face. You're pushing back against the misplacer beast with all of your strength, struggling to calculate your next move.

Your sword is in its sheathe and you're tempted to reach for it, but you're worried you won't be able to keep this frightening creature at bay with a single hand.

Give it everything you've got and push the beast off on page 159
Go for your sword on page 166

110

You consider this offer for a moment, then shift gears.

"You know what, it's fine," you reply, waving away the die. "Times change and that's okay. Right now I want to focus on the present."

As these words leave your mouth an eruption of battle cries begin to flood the cemetery, echoing joyfully across the misty scene. They're followed shortly after by the familiar clangs of sword and shield.

"I better get going," you continue. "I don't wanna miss this."

Chuck nods as you turn and take off running, sprinting back to your friends as a brand new adventure begins.

THE END

King Rolo reaches into his pocket, pulling out a dagger and placing it against the boy's throat. The crowd gasps, backing away in terror.

Fortunately, you suddenly remember the 'turn into frog' scroll that's been traveling with you since your days as a wizard.

Thinking fast, you pull out the scroll and begin to read, magical energy gradually swirling around you as your voice grows louder and louder. Green sparks begin to crackle and leap from these arcane rings, growing in size until eventually they erupt forth and strike King Rolo.

The sentient die cries out, signaling his guards to attack you, but before he can fully express this command his body begins to change. There's a loud sucking noise as the king abruptly shrinks, his body turning green as he transforms into a tiny amphibian.

He's now a frog.

Immediately, the townspeople erupt in an excited cheer, apparently just as thrilled as when they discovered treasure bags on their doorsteps. Before the guards have a chance to apprehend you, the citizens rush forward as an adoring crowd. They hoist you into the air and begin carrying you toward the castle.

To your amazement, the royal guards reluctantly fall into step behind them. Looks like *everyone* has had enough of King Rolo.

"Our leader!" someone cries out.

"A new master of the realm!" another screams.

As you continue toward the castle the mob only grows in size, a parade of adoring fans who are anxious for a new era in Billings. It's a thrilling sensation to be elevated like this, both figuratively and otherwise, but as the royal palace looms closer and closer, you can't help but feel strangely unhappy about the direction this is headed.

"Wait!" you cry out. "Stop! Put me down!"

The adoring crowd is difficult to control, but as you continue to plead they eventually slow. By the time you reach the front of the castle the mob puts you down, the whole parade of revelers stepping back and giving you enough space to speak.

You clear your throat, standing at the top of this hill and gazing out at a gathering of citizens who pack these streets from here to the city gate.

"I appreciate your love," you offer, "but the last thing Billings needs is another leader who got there through force."

The mob begins to murmur, glancing at one another in utter

112

confusion.

"Billings will no longer have kings or queens," you annouce. "I'll take charge for the time being, but *only* long enough to hold a fair election. The people of this kingdom deserve to have a say in who represent them. From this day forward, Billings will be a democracy!"

The whole crowd erupts in a cheer of excitement, thrilled by this startlingly fresh political concept.

You've suddenly found yourself with an incredible amount of work to do, but for the time being it'll have to wait. Today is a day for celebration.

THE END

Thinking fast, you turn around and begin heading back in the other direction. You keep your wits about you, but remain calm and collected. You're not sure what was lying in wait, but if you retreat now and reapproach from the shadows, you might be able to glean a little more information.

You continue walking until your sense of danger has entirely diminished. Here you wait, then eventually sneak off the road and into the cover of the thick forest. It's from this point of view you continue forward once more, getting the drop on whoever was hoping to do the same.

Your eyes are peeled and your ears sharp, focused on every little sound that emanates through the wilds around you.

Eventually, you begin to hear whispering coblin voices, a language you can't fully understand, but vaguely get the gist of.

Coblins are short, sentient corn on the cobs, a ruthless species of living objects who patrol this area in small war bands. They are carnivores, and enjoy the taste of human flesh on occasion. Thankfully, most of these roadside assaults are strictly for profit, small time bandit raids where they steal your items and take off into the forest.

This particular group of coblin bandits appear to be well armed, based on the soft clanking of their spears and clubs as they sit behind shrubs just a few feet off the trail.

You creep a little closer, catching sight of the mob. There's a small handful of these scrappy, sentient vegetables, about eight or nine of them.

Now that you're the one with the element of surprise, you feel like you could take them.

Wait until they leave before continuing on page 59
If you have the web scroll, use it to attack on page 106
Sneak attack with your staff of page 146

114

While it pains you to leave your *STEEL SWORD* behind, you're not one to underestimate the speed and tracking abilities of hungry misplacer beasts.

You leave the scene without hesitation, slinking off into the tall grass and immediately putting as much distance between you and the carnage as possible.

Unfortunately, this also means you have no tools to defend yourself on the journey ahead.

As you reach the edge of the golden fields, you glance down to find a long, sturdy stick. You pick it up and brush it off, snapping away a few renegade twigs until you've found yourself with a decent STAFF.

It's not much, but it'll have to do.

Your quest continues on page 76

"Yeah, Jorlin is being a jerk," you finally agree. "He's not considering the fact that everyone defines fun in their own way. Being free to do whatever you want isn't as great as it seems, because then there's no challenge."

"Exactly!" Lorbo blurts, finally shedding his quiet demeanor and allowing himself to get riled up a bit. "He doesn't get to decide what's fun and what isn't!"

You're nodding along, agreeing with your friend's frustrated diatribe in an attempt to be supportive.

"Having fun is the last thing that matters in a serious role-playing game!" Lorbo continues.

"Well, wait," you stammer. "You've gotta find a balance between the two, right?"

Lorbo scoffs. "You really think we can reach a compromise with a jerk like that?"

You realize suddenly this conversation has gone off the rails. You'd wanted to find common ground with your friend Lorbo, but now he's taking things a little too far. This kind of anger isn't going to bring the group any closer together.

In fact, it's doing the opposite.

Suddenly, the door opens behind you and Jorlin steps out onto the porch. "Ready to talk?" he questions.

Lorbo laughs. "If *you're* ready to apologize."

"I mean... not really," Jorlin counters.

You interject quickly, hoping to head this conversation off at the pass. "Hey! Can't we just find a middle ground?"

Lorbo glances over at you, confused, then rises and takes an aggressive stance. "Middle ground?" he blurts. "There's no reasoning with Jorlin. You said it yourself, the guys a total jerk."

"Hey," you stammer. "I wasn't... I didn't..."

Now, Jorlin is the one getting upset, shaking his head from side to side in utter disappointment. "So that's how it is?"

He's directing his question at you, but Jorlin jumps in to answer. "Yeah, that's how it is," he shouts, raising his voice to a previously uncharted volume. "Where the hell do you get off telling me the rules don't matter in my own house?"

"It's *our* game!" Lorbo counters.

"Not anymore," comes a voice from behind you.

The group turns to see Sarah standing in the doorway. She looks utterly exhausted, shaking her head from side to side in disappointment as she watches the three of you fight like paladins and rogues.

"This is too much," Sarah continues. "It's just not fun anymore if everyone's gonna be like this. Bad Boys and Buckaroos is about escaping the problems of the real world, not starting new ones."

Your first instinct is to immediately contradict her, to push for your group to stay together and keep playing like you always have, but for some reason you just can't get your mouth to form the words.

Maybe she's right.

"Guess that's the end, then," Lorbo finally replies. "You all should pack up and head home."

The future awaits on page 37

There's something about this riddle that seems vaguely familiar, the answer floating through the back of your mind like some subconscious connection to a distant timeline. You close your eyes for a moment, drawing on the knowledge of your other self.

Your mind is racing, calculating various ways of looking at this problem and then finally settling on your answer.

You open your eyes and press the button marked 'hit'.

There's a sharp clang, followed by a rapid ticking sound from within the safe. You freeze in place, not sure if these noises are a sign of utter disaster or a job well done.

You don't have to wait long to find out.

Suddenly, a powerful explosion tears through the room, the front of the safe blowing open with fiery magical energy and a flurry of metal shards. The eruption is so sudden that you barely have time to scream, your body disintegrating in a sweeping cascade of arcane energy.

THE END

"Sure," you reply, climbing out of your chair and strolling over next to him.

You sit down on the floor and take a look at some of the books, opening them up and scrolling through the pages. "Okay, this section is what kind of character you want to be," you explain. "You can be a wizard or a warrior or a true buckaroo."

As you say this, notes from your old session fall from the pages, tucked away for years and years like some glorious hidden treasure. You help Zippy get started, then open up your old scribblings and have a look.

Immediately, you're transported back to a time when your imagination ran wild, where you weren't afraid to get lost in the world of fantasy and ideas. You miss those days, and for a moment you're hit with a powerful wave of nostalgic sadness.

Gradually, however, that sadness fades. You glance over to see Zippy writing out the backstory of his character, excitedly rolling dice and marking in his various statistics.

"I think I'm almost ready," your nephew offers.

"Really?" you blurt, then glance down at your phone to check the time. You've been looking at your notes for quite a while.

"Okay then," you offer, finding a Tingle Master screen and propping it up between the two of you.

"Our journey begins in a glorious castle, where King Rolo has summoned you to fulfill a great prophecy," you announce. "You're standing in the main foyer, gazing up at the enormous stone arches that line these hallowed halls."

As you describe the setting, the walls of your own home fall away, replaced by the majestic Billings castle that you once knew so well. You're standing next to Zippy, who is now clad in a full suit of plate armor and gripping an enormous broadsword that is way too large for him.

"You there!" a heavily armored unicorn calls out, approaching your nephew swiftly. "Are you the peasant who was sent for training?"

Zippy nods.

"I am Lady Norbalo," the unicorn continues. "Come with me, let's get started."

You watch as the two of them leave, looking forward to the epic quests that lie ahead.

"Good job, buckaroo," comes a familiar voice from behind you.

You turn to find Chuck Tingle in his white robes and pink mask.

"Chuck!" you gush, giving him a warm hug. "I didn't think I'd ever see you again."

"It was looking pretty rough there for a minute," Chuck explains. "When you stopped imagining things, The Void swept across the land. Everything was destroyed."

"Looks pretty good to me," you retort, gazing around the massive castle.

"That's the thing about imagination," Chuck explains. "It only takes a little bit to get things back on track. There are all kinds of adventures left for Zippy, and this world will live on through him."

"I can't wait," you reply.

"Looks like you fulfilled the prophecy after all," Chuck offers warmly.

THE END

120

You feel drawn to the bazaar, heading off toward the hustling, bustling sea of revelers that fill these city streets. Every direction you look there's a new, exciting sight, a stand full of exotic, colorful fruits on one side of the lane while an assortment of strange fish are laid out on the other. There are carts selling weapons and armor, and shops overflowing with glorious oil paintings and ancient pottery.

Somewhere in the distance, a band is playing a gleeful jig, and you're drawn to the sound. Before you can get very far, however, a man calls out to stop you.

"You there!" comes the voice, barking at you over the din on the street.

You turn back to see a large bigfoot in beautiful yellow robes. He's standing behind a stall with an assortment of magical wands spread out before him on a luxurious purple cloth.

"Wands for sale," he offers. "Incredible magical effects that anyone can perform, and I mean *anyone!* Come give it a whirl!"

Keep walking to page 165
Try a wand on page 141

Your first instinct is to dive out of the way, but in the split second this massive beast takes to clamp its jaws down around you another defensive maneuver enters your mind. You flip your staff so that it's pointing straight up and down, a toothpick in comparison to the dragon's massive size. Still, a toothpick stuck in just the right place can cause a lot of trouble, and that's exactly what happens.

The enormous dragon grunts loudly as it attempts to shut its mouth, then becomes even more frustrated when opening wider still won't provide relief. The creature is certainly strong enough to shatter your wooden staff, but this little sliver is positioned in such a way that this would be extremely painful.

You're standing on the dragon's tongue now, surrounded by certain death as its enormous teeth lie to one side and a bubbling toxic pit of Voidal tar lies to the other.

You watch as the ooze begins to gurgle and churn, threatening to spew up and wash over you, but before the dragon has a chance to belch up this awful substance you cry out in protest.

"Wait!" you shout. "If you wash me in that ooze then you'll be stuck with a staff in your mouth until someone else comes along! You need me."

The Voidal tar stops bubbling and settles back down as the dragon lets out a frustrated sigh.

"Maybe I'll just leave you this way regardless," you continue, suddenly realizing your position of power. "I could walk out of here and this stick would stay lodged forever."

You stroll to the edge of the dragon's teeth and watch as the Voidal mess begins to bubble up again, then step back to your original position.

The unfortunate truth of the matter washes over you in a sickening wave. You're stuck with this dragon just as much as this dragon is stuck with you.

"Well, this is quite the standoff we've found ourselves in," you offer, sitting down on the creature's soft tongue.

You remain here for an hour or so, struggling to find a way out of this pickle. During this time the dragon shifts through a series of powerful emotions, from anger and frustration to calm acceptance.

It also gives you a moment to reflect, to consider the fact that this beast isn't quite as evil as you'd initially thought. The Void is a horrific abomination, but its influence over your opponent is nothing more than an infection.

The hours stretch on and on, and eventually you find yourself overwhelmed with sympathy for this frustrated, lonesome creature. The dragon and its Voidal influence are two totally different things, and there's gotta be a way to separate them.

Finally, you speak up. "Listen, I could stay here forever because I'm perfectly comfortable. Your tongue is soft and cozy, and I'm not the one with a toothpick stuck in my mouth," you explain, "but I don't wanna do that. I know you're not the one who wants to eat me, it's The Void that has control over you."

The dragon grunts in acknowledgement.

"I don't know much about The Void, but I *do* know one thing, it can't stand kindness and love," you explain. "So I'm about to do something kind for you. I'm going to take out this staff."

To your amazement, the color begins seeping back into the dragon's jet black scales. The creature is shifting into a dull grey, then saturating with rosy pink.

"You can do whatever you want after that," you offer, "but I think you'll do the right thing. I think a little kindness goes a long way."

You stand up and walk over to your staff, gripping it tightly.

"Hold on," you offer. "This might sting at first, but then everything's gonna feel so much better."

You shift your weight as you find the best angle, then give one sharp tug. The staff pops out and the dragon breathes a long sigh of relief.

Their jaws don't clamp down around you.

As you climb out of the creature's mouth, you notice the color of their scales continue to shift. They're now a brilliant neon pink.

"Thank you," the dragon gushes, tearing up a bit, "that was horrible. The Void is such an empty, lonely place, but your display of kindness brought me back."

"Glad I could help," you reply warmly.

"You know, I never considered how nice it feels to have someone working on your teeth like that, getting into all the nooks and crannies. You had a very gentle touch," the dragon admits.

"I didn't realize that's something dragons were looking for," you reply.

The pink dragon nods. "Oh yeah, we get things stuck in our teeth all the time."

These words resonate deeply within you, the seed of opportunity planted somewhere in the back of your mind. As much as you've enjoyed your journey as a warrior, you're also profoundly thankful no blood was spilled today.

"I came all the way out here to fulfill a warrior's prophecy," you finally state, talking more to yourself than the dragon, "but things didn't end the way I expected."

"Was the prophecy fulfilled?" the dragon questions.

You nod. "I think so. The Void is retreating, but it's not the power of the sword that did it. It's the power of love."

The two of you sit in silence for a while.

"Now what?" the dragon finally asks.

You laugh. "Tell me again how dragon's like getting their teeth cleaned."

It's this moment that marks the beginning of a beautiful friendship. You and the pink dragon, who's name you learn is Trevor, open up a dragon dentistry business that takes the kingdom by storm, putting these massive reptilian creatures in much better moods and saving countless lives.

All thanks to one little moment of kindness.

THE END

Without hesitation, you pull out your 'turn into frog' scroll and begin to read, briskly sweeping through the incantation before this dark sorcerer has time to stop you.

The dinosaur springs into action, rushing forward and raising their hands to fire off a bolt of magical energy. Unfortunately for Count Storb, their reaction time just isn't quick enough.

A surge of green crackling rings has already bloomed around you, growing in size and then launching out at your dinosaur attacker. The second Count Storb is struck by these rings he begins to shift and change, the body once capable of delicate and complex arcane movements becoming awkward and strange. The dinosaur collapses as he runs, his legs disappearing beneath him, and before the sorcerer hits the ground his frame has altered completely.

A small green frog now sits in the count's place, harmless and confused as the orange blaze continues to rise around you.

Thinking fast, you rush over and scoop up the tiny, frightened amphibian, tossing it into your bag and then sprinting back toward the front doors. Brick and wood cascades down, narrowly missing your head as throw yourself through the exit in a final escape.

As you splash into the swamp outside the whole building comes tumbling down behind you, collapsing in a plume of flame and ash.

Back in Billings a parade is thrown in your honor, and while your new room in the castle provides a spectacular view, you decide to go down and check out the festivities up close. This is *your* parade, after all, and the following feast will be something to remember.

With the prophecy fulfilled, The Void's influence has slowly dissipated across the land. Monsters are retreating into the wilds and peace is returning to the kingdom of Billings.

These days, it's hard to imagine the little frog on your desk causing so many problems.

You stroll over and check on his cage, making sure there's plenty of water to drink and grubs to eat.

"You gonna be okay in here while I check out the parade?" you ask the tiny amphibian.

The frog just stares at you, blinking a few times but otherwise unresponsive.

"I'll give you a nice view," you offer, picking up the cage and carrying it over to a window sill. "There you go."

With that, you head out to enjoy your day, fully accepting your place as a hero.

THE END

"Let's do it," you finally reply, accepting the path of the true buckaroo.

Chuck pats you lovingly on the back. "Dang! Good choice bud. You'll do a great job with that ol' prophecy, I just know it. Follow me!"

Your mysterious new friend makes a sharp turn off the main road and starts cutting his way through the wide open fields as you follow behind.

Eventually, the yellow plains and farmland gives way to the edge of a deep, lush forest. It's here you must keep your wits about you, a place where the monsters of the wilds are free to creep along and do their hunting. While you don't expect any Voidal creatures to have made it this far, there are still plenty of natural beasts who would love to have you as a meal.

"Do you feel like the great role-player?" Chuck questions as you push deeper into the wilds.

You consider his words for a moment. "I'm not sure. I mean, this morning I was just another citizen of Billings, now the fate of the world rests on my shoulders. That's a lot of power."

"Well, if it makes you feel any less heckin' stressed then you should know *everyone* has this power," the mysterious man explains. "Every action that we take creates infinite other timelines. This happens for each moment as you trot through your reality and it makes you so mighty it's hard to even think about. Question is, what are you gonna use this power for? When those other timelines split off are they gonna be better or worse?"

"Better," you reply confidently.

"That's the true buckaroo way," Chuck offers with a smile, patting you on the shoulder. "I think you're definitely cut out for this."

With that, the man in the white robes and pink bag motions for you to follow, then starts making his way deeper into the woods.

The two of you venture into this humming natural landscape of old-growth trees and thick carpets of soft green moss. Light shines through the scene in warm hazy shafts that illuminate a dim, canopied world. As you travel, it's difficult to remember this is actually a very dangerous place.

It's just so beautiful.

The longer you walk, the more the sun begins to creep its way across the sky. Soon enough, warm afternoon air transitions into the cool chill of the evening.

Eventually, the soft drone of chanting voices begins to echo out through the woods, growing louder with every step as a large stone temple comes into view. There are figures all over the structure, going about their business in service of some unknown mystical tradition. A few of them are hugging warmly while others carry supplies to and from the temple.

As you pass these robed true buckaroos they stop what they're doing and turn to greet you warmly.

"Love is real!" they offer.

"Love is real," you instinctively retort, prompting kind smiles from the crowd.

You head inside the temple and Chuck Tingle leads you to a small chamber, featuring a single window and a modest bed.

"Hiked a long way, buckaroo," the mysterious man offers. "You should get some rest. Big day tomorrow, bright and early we'll trot and prove love. That's when the journey really begins."

With that, Chuck leaves.

His observation was dead on, you're absolutely exhausted. You climb into bed and within a few minutes you've drifted off to sleep, curious what the next morning will bring.

Wake up on page 8

You accept the twenty sided die, rolling it gently in your hands as you get a sense of the weight. You immediately recognize this as the lucky die that Limber gave you back at the office, smiling as you perceive the subtle hum of its natural energy.

Still, this attempt is not a sure thing, and it's hard to ignore all the variations at play. Would it land on a twenty if you threw it right now? What if you waited another thirty seconds?

Of course, none of that really matters. There's no way to tell what lies around the corner, you've just gotta take your shot when you can.

You find a perfectly flat headstone, then carefully make your roll. You watch as the die bounces and tumbles, finally coming to rest on the absolute best result you could possibly imagine.

"Twenty!" you call out joyfully.

Suddenly, the sound of a digital ringing pulls you back into reality. You're sitting at the dining room table with your friends once again, and your cell phone is vibrating hard as it hums a familiar tune.

"Sorry about that," you blurt, feeling bad that you've managed to pull your friends out of the game along with you.

You grab your phone to put it on silent, but you happen to catch sight of the caller identification and it stops you in your tracks. Sarah is on the other end of the line, your former Tingle Master finally reaching out after all these years.

"I'm so sorry," you tell your friends. "I need to get this."

You answer the phone.

"Hello?" you offer.

"Hey, it's Sarah," comes a familiar voice on the other end. "I know this is a little out of the blue, but I've been talking to Lorbo and Jorlin and they mentioned wanting to get another game started.

You can't help but laugh, shocked at the way all of this has fallen into place. "This is so crazy," you admit. "I'm actually playing right now with a new group. You should all come over and join in."

Swords ring out through the graveyard as Limber, Gorb and Ashley battle their zombie bicycle adversaries. It's a tough first battle, and the adventuring party is starting to weaken. At this point, most of their abilities have been drained, and they find themselves making defensive maneuvers as they back away from the growing undead horde.

The heroes begin to exchange glances, realizing this game might be ending just as quickly as it started.

"Need a little help?" comes a confident tone.

The adventurers look up to see three new allies emerge over the top of a hill, their weapons drawn. Limbo, Jorlin and Sarah let out a powerful battle cry as they rush down to join the fray.

THE END

Realizing this might be your only chance to save the town, you take your shot. In a split second, you pull your staff back and swing as hard as you can at your companion.

Your weapon crackles with magical energy as it flies through the air, but it never has a chance to reach Amanda.

The bumblebeeholder is much too fast, firing a yellow bolt of energy that instantly vaporizes your body and leaves your staff to splash into the murky swamp below.

Amanda doesn't even bother to pick it up, turning around and fluttering off toward the nearby town.

Soon enough, screams begin to fill the air.

THE END

"I don't have anything!" you reply, throwing your hands up in a gesture of surrender.

"Nothing?" the lead coblin asks, tilting her head curiously to the side.

"I know you're out here trying to make a living as bandits, but it's only gonna work if I've got something for you to take," you continue as convincingly as possible. "You should let me keep walking so you can stop the next person to come through. Maybe *they'll* have magic items."

The coblins exchange disappointed glances, chattering amongst themselves in their chirping vegetable language.

"Can I go now?" you continue, growing frustrated.

The leader nods and the group begins to separate, pulling back their spears and lowering their clubs. However, you only get a few steps before the coblin leader cries out to stop you.

"Search!" she suddenly erupts.

The coblins raise their weapons again as one of them approaches you. He begins to pull at your bag as you struggle to keep it away from him.

"Give!" the leader screams, the spears pushing in even closer now.

Finally, you relent, handing over your bag and revealing the arcane scrolls held within.

"Lies!" the lead coblin shrieks. "Lies! Evil! Kill!"

"Whoa, whoa, whoa!" you blurt, waving your hands in the air, nobody need to kill-"

Before you can finish the sentence, you feel a sharp pain in your side. You glance down to see that one of their long, sharp spears has been thrust into you, slipping between your ribcage and puncturing one or more vital organs.

More spears are suddenly thrust into your flesh. You cry out and stumble back, struggling to get away, but your body is already too for much of a fight. Blood spills forth as you collapse to the ground, struggling to breath as the coblins scream joyfully around you.

The last thing you see before the world fades to black is the coblin leader excitedly pulling things out of your bag.

THE END

You decide to approach the plucky young intern Gorb, recognizing that a little excitement can go a long way when trying to get a tabletop role-playing group off the ground.

Gorb doesn't have a cubicle of his own yet, just spends the day running back and forth through the office as he struggles to maintain a cascade of pithy requests. He seems a bit overwhelmed at the moment, which gives you pause, but when Gorb spots you approaching he immediately breaks out in a wide smile.

"What's going on?" he questions. "Need me to run a grab you some chocolate milk?"

You shake your head. "Not today," you reply. "I'm actually starting a Bad Boys and Buckaroos group. It's a tabletop role-playing game with dragons and swords and stuff."

Gorb nods along. "Cool. Sounds like you'll have a lot of fun."

The two of you stand awkwardly for a moment before you realize what's happening.

"Oh, I mean... I want you to come play," you finally blurt. "I'm asking you to join us."

The intern's eyes go wide. "Wait, really? Me?"

"Of course!" you reply happily.

"I'd love to!" Gorb continues. "I've never played before, but it sounds like a blast. I've heard Limber plays, too."

Overhearing her name, Limber glances up from her work and looks over at you.

"That true?" you question. "Do you play Bad Boys and Buckaroos?"

Limber nods, saying nothing but clearly interested.

"You wanna join our new game?" you ask.

Limber nods again. "We can play at my place this evening."

As you head back to your desk, you find yourself overwhelmed with excitement at how well everything just fell into place. It's been years since you set foot in that fantasy world, and you can't wait to get started.

The first game of your new group is tonight.

Game night awaits on page 52

You try your best to dive out of the way, but the massive reptilian monster is simply too fast. The creature has taken you off guard, allowing you to think it was weakened well beyond the actual state of its exhaustion, and this tiny mistake has cost you everything.

You cry out as the massive beast bites your leg and tosses you across the cavern like a rag doll. You slam into the far wall, shattering every bone in your body, then struggling to crawl away despite the pain.

Behind you, the dragon begins to vomit forth a horrible cascade of bubbling Voidal tar, the black ooze creeping across the ground just slightly faster than you can pull yourself away from it.

Soon enough, the cosmic tar is washing over you, covering your body and consuming your mind.

THE END

134

It gradually occurs to you that the spaghetti is only necessary if you encounter this notorious guard dog, but if you avoid him entirely then you'll be just fine. This plan was a good one before a knife wielding bigfoot chef was blocking your path, but now it's time to roll with the punches.

There's just too much risk.

You pull back, slinking away from the kitchen and returning to the castle's main foyer. Here, you begin to creep your way up the large staircase in utter silence. You're like a ghost, a phantom of the night who will avoid even the most scrutinizing efforts of detection.

Once reaching the upper level, you being to make your way down a series of long, twisting hallways.

Sneak along to page 55

You hoist your staff and sprint toward Count Storb, facing your opponent head on as the fire rages around you.

The dinosaur moves to meet you halfway, raising his hands and blasting forth a bolt of crackling necromantic energy from his fingertips. You immediately use your staff to block this surge of arcane power, and for the most part it works. Your staff receives the brunt of this power surge, consuming the lighting before it has a chance to affect you, but it quickly becomes apparent this will only work so many times.

You reach the dinosaur and swing your weapon, slamming into him as a brilliant flash of orange energy fills the room. Count Storb is pushed backward by this monumental attack, but he stays on his feet, sliding across the ground as he braces himself against the magical force.

The stegosaurus raises his hands and blasts forth another surge of dark magic, only amplified by its deep connection to the endless cosmic Void. Again, you raise your staff to defend yourself, but now your weapon has been significantly weakened. Still, it somehow manages to takes the force of this arcane bolt.

You realize now that your time is running out. You charge at the sorcerer, sprinting through the burning foyer and putting all of your power into a single forceful swing. The staff comes whipping around and strikes the dinosaur in the side, erupting with a blast of brilliant orange energy.

Count Storb screams as he's blown in half, the two pieces of his body flipping through the air in a shower of orange sparks. The separate halves land with a thud in the roaring fires that swiftly consume this building.

You've slain the dark sorcerer, and with this task completed a wave of relief washes over you. Still, there's no time to relax.

As the structure continues to crumble you turn around and run for the exit. Brick and wood cascades down around you, narrowly missing your head as throw yourself through the front doors of the tower in a final escape.

As you splash into the swamp outside the whole building comes tumbling down behind you, collapsing in a plume of flame and ash.

The expression on Grimble's face when he opens the door to greet you is a beautiful mixture of emotions. He's shocked, thankful, and proud, opening his large bigfoot arms and giving you a powerful hug.

"You did it," the wizard offers. "The Void is already losing its grip on this land. The monsters are withdrawing into the wilderness once more and peace has returned to the kingdom."

"I couldn't have done it without your training," you reply.

Grimble the Grey smiles. "That's exactly why I called you here. You brought your staff?"

You nod, handing over your weapon.

"Good," the bigfoot continues. "You've earned yourself an upgrade."

Grimble takes your staff and places it on a magical rack, the wooden stick held in place as he begins a special incantation. You watch as the crackling orange energy flows through your weapon, dancing spastically across its length in glorious electric crackles.

The rack itself begins to hum, pouring forth a magical energy of its own. It's not long before these two distinct forces begin to mix, and suddenly the whole contraption erupts in a shower of brilliant sparks.

Even Grimble jumps back in alarm, thrilled by this majestic arcane display.

As soon as the energy settles he picks up your ORANGE STAFF and hands it back to you, your weapon now buzzing with crimson surges of power. You accept the RED STAFF, gazing down at this mighty artifact with a deep reverence.

"This is incredible," you gush, "but my quest is over. It's an honor to possess such a powerful weapon, but what's the point if I don't get to use it."

Grimble shrugs. "You earned it," the bigfoot offers. "Just enjoy it."

You grip the staff tight, feeling it's energy hum through your body as a smile works its way across your face.

THE END

Your body surges with adrenaline as the instinct to run overwhelms you. Without a second thought, you spin abruptly and take off running, causing the guard dog to erupt in a fury of snapping jaws and frantic barks.

Soon enough, you're sprinting back through the hallways from which you came, a ferocious beast nipping at your heels and swiftly gaining speed. You quickly realize your initial calculations were off, and you'll never be able to outrun this canine. Trying to get away is just delaying the inevitable.

You're toast.

You consider falling to the ground and hoping this creature has been trained to restrain its prey, rather than gobble them up for dinner, but before you have a chance something truly unexpected happens.

A hand reaches out from the darkness and grabs you by the collar as you sprint past them, yanking you back into the shadows. Before you have a chance to collect your bearings you realize the wall is spinning around and sealing tight with a loud thud, transporting you into a part of the castle that's typically hidden from view.

Standing before you is the man who provided this sudden trapdoor rescue, a mysterious figure in stark white robes and sporting a pink bag over his head. The words "love is real" are written across the front of the man's mask.

"You saved me," you breathlessly gush, nearly collapsing from exhaustion. "Thank you."

"Sure thing, buckaroo," the man offers. "Didn't seem like it was your time to go just yet. Lots of dead ends on this journey, but every once and a while a bud deserves a second chance."

"Who are you?" you question.

"Chuck Tingle," the man explains. "Just thought I'd stop by to tell you that your dang prophecy is much bigger than you think."

"I've been hearing that a lot," you admit.

"Well, it's heckin' true, bud. You might feel like a warrior or a wizard or a sneak, but deep down you're a true buckaroo at heart. Your journey is much more important than feedin' spaghetti to some dang dog."

"Then what *is* my journey?" you question, finally catching your breath.

"Come on, bud," Chuck offers, motioning for you to follow him. "I'll show you."

Soon enough, the two of you are creeping your way through a labyrinth of secret passages that twist their way through the dungeons and sewers of this enormous kingdom. Your trek begins within the castle walls, but eventually you realize you've traveled far beyond the royal grounds. In fact, it's tough to tell if you're still inside the city at all.

"How did the sneak's guild not know about these tunnels?" you question.

"They're still part of the game," Chuck explains. "That has limitations. True buckaroos play outside the game, bud. Are you ready to trot path of the true buckaroo and prove love is real?"

"I... think so," you reply.

"Well dang!" Chuck replies excitedly. "Sounds like a plan, bud."

Chuck reaches a set of stairs that lead upward, ending at a wooden trap door in the stone ceiling. The mysterious man pushes on this hidden door once, twice, three times as dirt crumbles down around him. Finally, Chuck erupts outward in a shower of soil and pebbles, revealing the night sky and a crisscross of thick branches above.

You climb out to discover your instincts were correct. You're now deep in the forest, surrounded by thick shrubbery and ferns while old growth trees tower over you. Moonlight slips through the scene in warm hazy shafts that illuminate this dim, canopied world.

"Let's go, buckaroo," Chuck coaxes as he leads you onward.

Eventually, the soft call of chanting voices echoes out through the woods, growing louder with every step we take until, eventually, a large stone temple comes into view. There are figures all over the structure, going about their business in service of some mystical tradition you're unaware of. Some of them are hugging warmly while others carry supplies to and from the temple.

As you pass these robed true buckaroos they all stop what they're doing, then turn to you and greet you warmly.

"Love is real!" they all offer.

"Love is real," you instinctively retort, prompting warm smiles from the crowd.

You head inside the temple and Chuck Tingle leads you to a tiny chamber, which features a single window and a small bed.

"Almost got eaten by a dang dog then hiked all night," the mysterious man observes. "You should get some rest. Big day tomorrow, bright and early we'll trot and prove love. That's when the journey *really* begins."

With that, Chuck leaves.

His observation was dead on, you're absolutely exhausted. You climb into bed, and within a few minutes you've drifted off to sleep, curious what the next morning will bring.

Wake up on page 8

140

It's been a long road to get here, but now that you're standing before this frightening dark sorcerer you realize you're just not cut out for the job. Coblins and zombies were one thing, but an opponent this powerful is something else entirely.

"Are you ready... to die?" the dinosaur bellows, his powerful voice reverberating through the walls around you.

"Actually, I'm just gonna run away," you call back.

Count Storb hesitates, confused. "Wait, what?"

"Yeah, I'm just gonna run," you offer.

"You don't want to fight an epic final battle?" the stegosaurus continues.

"No thanks," you offer.

"But, look at all this bad ass fire?" Count Storb replies, growing frustrated as he motions around the room. "The stage is set."

"Not for me, though," you reply.

"You can't jus-" the dinosaur begins, but before he gets the chance to finish you've turned abruptly and ran for the door.

You make it two steps before a powerful bolt of necromantic energy slams into you. It vaporizes your body in a cascade of swirling darkness and shrieking skulls.

THE END

You give into temptation and approach the bigfoot, stepping up to his booth of wands and giving these powerful magic items a closer look. There are all kinds of scams at play here in the market, so you're sure to keep your wits about you, but the friendly demeanor of this yellow robed bigfoot immediately puts you at ease.

"Welcome to Melovan the Magnificat's Wand Emporium," the bigfoot offers enthusiastically. "Here we specialize in wands that anyone can use, even you!"

The wizard is talking so loudly that a crowd has started to gather, an assortment of marketgoers gathering around to see what's the commotion. You get the feeling this whole thing is actually part of a larger sales pitch, a way to drive business that has less to do with you and more to do with all these excited voyeurs. Still, you go with it.

Melovan picks up a wand from his display table and hands it over to you. "We call this the crackler," he explains. "It's a simple display, like holding a beautiful bouquet of flowers in your hand. Do you think you can handle that?"

You nod.

"Alright," the bigfoot confirms. "Now, wrap your fingers tightly around the wand and point in upward. When you activate it's powers, you'll feel a slight kickback. Not to worry, the plume of sparks will be no larger than two feet."

"How do I activate its powers?" you question.

"Just say that magic word: *gygaxalon!*"

You hold the wand out as instructed, pointing it up and away from the crowd as you focus your energy. You close your eyes and try your best to summon forth the magical power within you, connecting to the faint tremble and pulse of the natural world. You feel a slight tingle run from the bottom of your feet to the tip of your fingers, coalescing in the wand held tight in your hand.

At least, you *think* you feel it. You've never actually done this before.

"*Gygaxalon!*" you cry out, taking your shot.

The second this magical phrase leaves your lips a huge, colorful plume of green energy erupts from the end of your wand. It blasts much farther than the few feet the wizard assured, illuminating the entire market with its brilliant, crackling presence.

The whole crowd gasps loudly, stepping away in shock as their eyes remain transfixed on your glorious display.

When the sparks finally settle, the gathering breaks out into a wild round of applause. You turn and hand the wand back over to Melovan, suddenly noticing the shocked look on his face.

"Pretty good," you offer.

"Pretty good?" the wizard repeats back in confusion. "That was ten times the display I was expecting. You've got magic in your blood."

You shrug. "I guess so."

"No, you don't understand," Melovan continues. "I've never seen anything like that. There's a prophecy telling of a wizard like yourself, someone with a deep natural talent that would pull the kingdom back from darkness."

"I've recently been made aware," you reply.

Melovan picks up on your slight disdain for the idea, but he decides to counter it by being direct. "You should really follow the path of magic and spell craft," the bigfoot offers encouragingly. "There's a great wizard I'd like you to meet. I can take you now."

You consider his offer, recognizing just how seriously Melovan is taking your magical prowess. Your display was good enough to bring him a landslide of new customers, but he's still willing to shut down the shop and escort you to this mighty wizard.

Maybe you really *are* meant for a path of magic and sorcery.

Go with Melovan to page 212
Decline on page 62

Without a second thought you turn and sprint as fast as you can into the grass, ducking down to keep your head from breaking the surface of this endless yellow field.

Your breathing heavy, you focus on working your arms and legs to push deeper into this golden expanse.

You hear a blood-curdling howl ring out across the field, followed shortly by the tense tones of rustling grass. The creature is enormous, but stealthy, so the cacophony of heavy paws slamming the ground is nowhere to be found as it races after you,. Still, you can feel it following close behind, sense this powerful hunter closing in on its wounded prey.

You push onward, forcing yourself to keep sprinting until it feels like your lungs are going to explode within your chest. When you just can't take it anymore you collapse to the ground, struggling to stay quiet despite your heavy breathing.

You make yourself as small as possible, then wait.

Gradually, the seconds become minutes, time stretching on and on while the misplacer beast is nowhere to be found. You realize slowly that, through some strange twist of fate, you've managed to escape the creature.

Unfortunately, you've left *ALL ITEMS* behind, rendering yourself completely defenseless on the journey to come.

As you climb to your feet and continue on your way, you find a long, study stick that can be used as a STAFF in combat. It's not the mightiest weapon out there, but it'll have to do.

Your quest continues on page 76

Hoping to tie up any loose ends you take off after the single coblin, following into the woods as it scrambles away. You duck and dodge through the undergrowth, weaving in and out of the trees as you struggle to keep this living corn on the cob in your line of sight.

You're sprinting as fast as you can, desperately trying to maintain your focus but finding it more and more difficult with every passing second. As soon as it feels like you're gaining on your target, the coblin will zip off in another direction and disappear into the thick forest.

Suddenly, however, keeping up with this scampering creature is the least of your worries.

You take a single misplaced step and suddenly feel a sharp tug on your leg. The branch above you springs upward as a rope tightens hard around your ankle, lifting you into the air in a shower of leaves.

You've been caught, dangling upside down with your head some four feet above the ground. You try your best you curl up and untie the knot around your ankle, but it's no use. You're stuck.

As a quiet falls upon the forest, a soft rustling fills your ears. You gaze out into the undergrowth to see the coblin you'd been chasing emerge from the woods.

The creature is furious, anger and hate boiling over from its eyes. He didn't enjoy getting chased down like that, not to mention what you did to his friends.

The creature lifts his spear, ready to impale you, but before he gets the chance an object comes barreling out of the woods. It's moving so fast you can barely see it, but your ears fill with a loud buzzing sound and you catch sight of a stark yellow and black pattern.

The coblin cries out, howling in pain while clutching his back as he falls to the ground in excruciating pain. The corn on the cob's shrieks sound absolutely horrific, gradually transforming into a strange gurgle and then eventually plummeting into silence as the vegetable collapses face down into the dirt.

Hovering in the air before you is a bumblebeeholder, a mythical creature you've heard about many times but never actually seen with your own eyes. The monster is similar to a large, perfectly round bumblebee, about three feet across and hovering in the air thanks to a comically small set of wings attached to her back. The body of the bee is covered in yellow and black stripes, and there's a large stinger on her tail end.

It appears this stinger is what killed the coblin.

The most notable feature of the bumblebeeholder, however, is that fact that her body is almost entirely made up of a single, enormous eye.

This giant ball gazes at you with a genuine curiosity.

"What are you doing up there?" the bumblebeeholder questions.

"I got caught in a trap," you retort. "Mind helping me down?"

The creature gazes at the rope that connects your ankle to the tree branch above. You watch as a magical energy begins to course through her body, coalescing within her pupil and then blasting out as a ray of arcane light. The brilliant yellow laser erupts forth and severs the rope instantly, causing you to fall to the ground with a loud thud.

You stand up and brush yourself off. "What's your name?" you question.

"Amanda," the bumblebeeholder replies. "Are you a wizard?"

You nod.

"The robes gave you away," she continues. "I can do some magic myself. All bumblebeeholders can."

"I can see that," you reply.

"Are you on some kind of *wizard mission?*" the monster asks excitedly.

You nod.

"Can I come?" she continues. "Wizard stuff is so cool."

You consider this for a moment, not quite sure how to answer. It appears this creature could be a powerful ally in battle, but you've only just met her and who knows if this is someone you can actually trust.

Of course, Amanda has already done plenty to prove herself. If it wasn't for her, you'd be skewered and roasting over the fire by now.

"I can be your *familiar!*" the bumblebeeholder suddenly blurts. "That's a thing, right? Like, a creature who acts as a wizard's assistant?"

If you'd rather go on your own turn to page 174
Allow the bumblebeeholder to join you on page 14

146

You decide to put your magical staff to good use, relying on your training as you spring forth from the bushes and deliver a devastating surprise attack to three of the coblins. You whip your staff around and swing it like a bat, slamming into the sentient vegetables and sending them flying with a surge of magical blue energy. The rest of the creatures spring into action, scrambling to gather their weapons, but you're much too fast.

You dive and roll, then take another swing with your staff that hits one of the creatures so hard it erupts in a flash of light. It's body scatters across the trail in a torrent of yellow popcorn.

One of the coblins comes running at you from behind, his club raised, but you realize he's there well before he has a chance to take a swing. You thrust you staff backward, tearing through yet another opponent with a brilliant flash.

It's not long before the whole mob has been dispatched, either lying face down in the dirt as blood pools around them, or heated with your magic stuff until they erupt in a shower of popcorn.

As you stand over your fallen opponents you can feel the magical energy that flows within you blossoming. The arcane forces that arc with blue lightening shift in hue, your *BLUE STAFF* fading away as it's replaced by an ORANGE STAFF of even greater power.

It's just as you suspected, the journey itself is proving to be an important part of your training.

You take a moment to wipe the dirt away from your robes, then continue onward.

Resume the journey on page 17

Thinking fast, you rush over and grab the sharpened bone segment.

Now armed, you begin to push back into the troll's space, lunging forward with your weapon then pulling back every time he swipes in return. It takes a while for an opportunity to show itself, but eventually you spot your opening.

You rush the beast and stab him with your large bone shard, causing a horrible cry to erupt from the monster's throat. Unfortunately, regardless of how well placed your blow is, it does little to slow the troll down.

The creature wraps his arms around you and pulls you toward him, opening his jaws wide and then snaping them down around your head.

The last thing you see is several rows of teeth surrounding your field of vision, a sharp pain in the neck as your head is torn away from your body and hungrily swallowed.

THE END

King Rolo reaches into his pocket, pulling out a dagger and placing it against the boy's throat.

The crowd gasps, backing away in terror.

Your first instinct is to rush the king and his royal guards, to throw yourself into battle and save this child, but as the soldiers draw their weapons you realize there's no way out of this one. Another step forward and it'll be lights out for both you and the boy.

You feel helpless, overwhelmed with anger and frustration. After all of that effort to fulfill the prophecy and return what rightfully belonged to the citizens of Billings, you've found yourself trapped. You won the game, but King Rolo doesn't play by the rules.

The tension within you finally bubbles up and spills out of your mouth, erupting from your throat in an unexpected cry.

"Boo!" you shout, a lone voice carrying over the crowd.

The King and his guards look at you, astounded by the gall on display.

Gradually, however, more voices begin to rise from the angry mob.

"You're the worst!" someone shouts. "Get out, King Rolo!"

"He's no king of mine!" someone adds.

Soon enough, the whole crowd is booing and hissing, crying out to express their overwhelming frustration.

In all this chaos, the young boy slips away from King Rolo's grip. He disappears into the crowd.

This overwhelming negativity finally gets to the king, his expression faltering as he realizes just how powerful the rage against him really is. His desire to push back against the mob crumbles, the weight of their anger finally forcing its way into the depths of his cold heart.

"Alright!" King Rolo blurts. "You can keep the money."

The crowd quiets down as he says this, but the king's announcement clearly doesn't draw the reaction he expected. Even with this swift reversal, nobody is cheering.

"Go back to your castle," someone yells. "Get the heck out of here!"

King Rolo lowers his head and turns around, making his way back up the cobblestone street as his royal guards follow behind.

Once the king disappears, the celebration begins again.

THE END

150

"Maybe later," you offer, then turn back toward the television and settle into your chair a little deeper.

You let out a long sigh, allowing the flickering images to wash over you. While Bad Boys and Buckaroos had once been an escape, your new way to disconnect is by sitting in front of the TV for hours. Honestly, it doesn't matter what's on, just so long as that soft digital hum is flooding your surroundings and washing over your brain like bleach.

Eventually you realize several hours have passed, and the news report has turned into a haunting display of dancing black and white static. You try getting up, but you feel too exhausted to move.

"Zippy?" you call out, your voice echoing through the empty home.

Has it really been a few hours, or has it been longer? You're starting to second guess the time that you've been stuck in this chair, noticing the aging features of your arms and legs. Maybe it's been years.

Hell, maybe it's been decades.

A loud bubbling sound draws your attention back to the television. You watch as black ooze begins to pour forth from the screen, spilling over the edge and running down to the floor in long, dark streaks. As the static hum grows louder, a pool of thick Voidal ooze begins to grow as the base of your entertainment center.

The closer this puddle of black tar creeps toward you, the more you begin to panic, but you now realize you're stuck firmly in place. You can't escape, regardless how desperately you try to free yourself from the confines of this furniture prison.

"Help!" you cry out, the black ooze sputtering forth from the television faster and faster.

The room is beginning to fill with this dark liquid, and as it finally reaches your skin you find yourself truly understanding how much you've missed out on. There's nothing to be found within this shiny black tar, an endless expanse of nothingness that you've created for yourself. After years of denying your own imagination, this is all that's left.

You let out one final scream as the black ooze rises above your head, flooding into your throat.

THE END

You run toward the guard, waving as you approach.

"Hey!" you cry out. "There's been an accident with your family! Someone's hurt!"

The eyes of the stegosaurus go wide with alarm. "Who is it?"

Say "your brother" on page 223
Say "your mother' on page 60

"Oh nothing," you finally offer. "I was just trying to figure out how I'm going to file these reports."

Ashley laughs. "Well, make sure you look a little busier if Krimble comes walking through, okay?"

You nod, prompting your friend to continue on her way.

As you get back to work, the little spark of imagination that had been bubbling up within you settles once more, flickering out just as quickly as it arrived. Before you know it, you've forgotten about any distant fantasy realms, focused instead on the world of timecards and spreadsheets that lies directly before you.

It's years before that spark ever returns.

Time passes, and soon enough you're not even working in the same position. You filter through a few jobs and eventually end up somewhere that's much less soul sucking, but you still find yourself living a very grounded and practical life.

One evening, you end up watching after your eleven year old nephew while his parents are out of town, stuck in the role of babysitter. Zippy was dropped off at your house no more than an hour ago, and the kid is already starting to get under your skin.

You're trying to watch the news, your eyes trained on the living room TV, but your nephew just keeps getting in the way. Of course, *you* remember having energy like that, but these days it would take a long to get you buzzing around the house like Zippy is.

"Can you just... sit still?" you question, "or at least stay out of the way if you're gonna keep running around?"

Your nephew seems extremely defeated by this comment, but he heeds your words. Zippy slinks off with a solemn expression plastered across his face.

You watch the television a little longer, then turn back to your nephew when you start to feel bad about your tone.

"Hey, I'm sorry I raised my voice like that," you begin, then stop when you notice the set of polyhedral dice Zippy holds in his hands.

You realize now that he's gonna into your closet, pulling forth your old role-playing books and supplies.

"What's this?" Zippy questions.

As much as you'd love to give him a straight answer, you immediately realize this inquiry will only lead to another, then another, and another.

You haven't thought about Bad Boys and Buckaroos for years. It could certainly end up being a fun walk down memory lane, but explaining the game is also a hell of a time commitment.

Say "nothing" on page 164
Tell him it's Bad Boys and Buckaroos on page 68

154

As you slash away at this ferocious beast the sword in your hand grows with power. The magical energy that courses through your sizzling blade begins to arc and leap, dancing across your weapon in a visual manifestation of your mighty power as a warrior. All of your training has come down to this.

Unfortunately, that power is not quite enough to break through the dragon's tough hide.

You let out a desperate cry, pulling your brilliant blue sword back for one final blow when, suddenly, the dragon lunges forward and snaps its massive jaws around you.

The next thing you know you're tumbling down the creature's throat, toxic fumes of The Void filling your nostrils. You realize that you'll splash into a pool of the toxic ooze within seconds, and make once last attempt at victory.

With a final slice, you tear through the dragon's throat from the inside out, erupting from its body in a slash of blue light. The monster lets out a deafening screech that rumbles through the cavern as you tumble forth, scrambling away as a cascade of simmering tar comes rushing after. It spills out and pools around the reptilian beast.

Color begins to seep into the dragon's scales once again, saturating from black, to grey, to a bright pink.

On the trek back to Billings you notice the natural world shares this same brilliant alteration, colors appearing slightly more vibrant as The Void loses its grip.

The kingdom celebrates your return, citizens dancing in the street and a parade thrown in your honor. The city now has more chocolate milk than it knows what to do with, and it's not long before this sweet brown treat becomes the official beverage of Billings.

Lady Norbalo couldn't be prouder of the warrior you've become, but your training quickly ends. Your martial skills have evolved past any of her lessons, and the only choice is to take up a new mantel. It's time for you to become the teacher, to open your own warrior training academy.

It's time for the next generation of adventurers to rise up and take on The Void for themselves.

THE END

You've spent way too much time planning this mission to change course now. Just because there's someone in the kitchen, it doesn't mean you won't be able to get what you came for. You're an expert sneak, after all.

You slowly creep toward the doorway, dropping down into a crouch as you peer around the corner and get a read on the scene. Sure enough, a bigfoot chef is working away on some nobel's midnight snack, moving back and forth as they gather ingredients and craft a late night meal.

It's a chocolate milk pie, and it smells delicious.

Fortunately, this culinary sasquatch is positioned on the other side of the room, and while you're certainly in their potential line of sight, the distance between you gives a distinct advantage.

A hearty portion of notorious castle spaghetti rests on the countertop next to you, laid out on a fancy plate just waiting to be served. Once again, your courage is put to the test. You're so close to this special pasta, but reaching up and snatching the plate is a difficult maneuver.

You peek around the corner once again, taking note of an enormous kitchen knife that's currently gripped by the late night bigfoot chef.

Go for the spaghetti on page 66
Continue on without the spaghetti on page 134

"You're not gonna like what I have to say," you finally offer, "but it's the truth. You and Lorbo are *both* pretty extreme in your opinions on this, and I think the real answer is finding a balance between the two. A great game of Bad Boys and Buckaroos is going to be fun, but it's also going to have structure. If one of those things leans to hard in either direction, then the whole thing will crash and burn."

"Well, I think our middle grounds might be too far apart," Jorlin counters. "That guy's never gonna compromise."

"That's another way the game can crash and burn," you continue, "if nobody's willing to give."

"I'm willing!" Jorlin blurts.

You gaze at him skeptically, saying nothing and allowing him to bask in this moment. The longer his assertion hangs in the air, the more ridiculous it begins to sound.

Finally, Jorlin lets out a long sigh. "Okay, maybe you're right," he offers. "Come on, let's get something at the corner store and head back."

The two of you continue into the night, strolling along until eventually arriving at a small convenience store. As you push through the doorway a bell jingles, announcing your arrival.

Jorlin knows exactly what he wants, grabbing a cold chocolate milk from the refrigerated section and carrying it up to the counter. You don't get anything for yourself, but as you approach your friend he points to a glass display case featuring an assortment of scratch-off lottery tickets.

"I need something to take my mind off all this," Jorlin explains. "Which one should I get?"

"Is *neither* an option?" you question. "That's a huge waste of money."

Jorlin laughs. "Come on, let's roll the dice."

You gaze at this assortment of multicolored squares, each one of them promising huge piles of cash and once-in-a-lifetime prizes. It's hard to decide which ticket feels the best to you, but eventually you narrow it down to a pair of options.

One card features a twisted background of pasta and marinara sauce, the noodles swirling together under an assortment of evenly placed meatballs. The title of this selection is 'Spaghetti For Life.'

The other ticket is more straightforward, featuring a shirtless muscular man with four treasure chests stacked upon his shoulders. He's handsome and smiling, egging you on to make this selection and change your life. This ticket features the title 'Billings Big Bucks.'

Pick Spaghetti For Life on page 196
Pick Billings Big Bucks on page 92

158

Seeing your chance, you decide to go for the dragon's soft underbelly. You rush toward the creature and courageously swing away as the it holds a battered eye with its protective claw.

Your weapon strikes its target again and again with little effect, but still you push onward, struggling to make any headway in your assault on this massive beast.

If you have the steel sword or the staff turn to page 198
If you have the blue sword turn to page 154
If you have the orange sword turn to page 75

You muster all the strength you can, focusing your energy as you push this monstrous canine up and away from your body. Your training has paid off, because you're actually making some headway, but before you get a chance to toss this ferocious misplacer beast to the side it lashes out with a tentacle and slices open your arm with an array of sharp barbs.

The wound isn't deep, but it's more enough to make you cry out in shock and lose your focus. You pull back and the monster uses this moment to strike, snapping its jaws down right next to the space that your head once occupied. Fortunately, you saw this move coming from a mile away and have managed to roll out from under the misplacer beast.

There's only a few seconds to collect yourself as the creature turns and prepares another lunge. In this time, however, you catch sight of your lost sword. It's leaning against the base of the nearby tree.

Of course, as your ferocious opponent prepares its next attack you're made keenly aware it might be wiser to turn and run.

This tall grass could be the key to your escape.

Run away to page 13
Grab your sword and fight on page 167

160

You decide to approach Limber and ask her to join your group. Of course, it's difficult to play a table top role-playing game if you have trouble speaking up, but at the end of the day what really matters is your power of imagination. From the few times you've interacted with Limber, you can tell that she's very cool and has an open mind.

You approach Limber's cubicle, knocking gently on the wall to announce your presence. She looks up at you curiously, but says nothing.

"Hey, I know this might seem a little out of the blue, but I'm putting together a Bad Boys and Buckaroos group. It's a tabletop role-playing game. Have you heard of it?

Limber nods.

"Do you want to play?"

Limber nods again, then reaches down and opens up the bag resting under her desk. She reveals her player's handbook and a bag full of dice. "I love Bad Boys and Buckaroos," she replies, finally speaking up.

Your eyes go wide, impressed by her collection. "Amazing!"

Limber reaches into her bag and pulls forth a single green die. She hands it over to you. "Thanks for asking me to play. It's been a while," she continues. "Have my LUCKY DIE."

You accept this gesture and thank your co-worker for her kindness.

Suddenly, Gorb the intern appears behind you. "Did someone say Bad Boys and Buckaroos?" he blurts. "I've always wanted to play."

You can't help but laugh. "You wanna join the game we're starting?" you question. "The more the merrier."

"First game tonight at my place!" Limber offers.

Game night awaits on page 52

You consider this for a moment, weighing the question in your mind.

Sure, rules are important, but at the end of the day does it really matter what the character's stats are or if they *really* strike with their magic sword? It feels like rules and regulations are just slowing down the enjoyment.

"I don't think we need to lean heavy on the guidelines," you finally offer in return. "Having fun is paramount."

Sarah's expression flickers slightly as you say this, but she maintains a smile. She's trying to listen with an open mind, but there's no question she disagrees with your sentiment.

Your friend is working something over in the depths of her mind, sorting through her beliefs as she synthesizes an appropriate response. She takes a deep breath and then slowly lets it out, as though finally accepting something that's been weighing her down for a very, very long time.

"I have to admit, I haven't had much fun being the Tingle Master lately," she says.

"Oh," you blurt, a little surprised. "Really? The game is moving along nicely, we just talked to the king and set out on a quest. It's getting good!"

Sarah just shakes her head. "Yeah, I know. I'm glad you all like the storyline, but it's still pretty exhausting for me to keep things fun without any structure. It's difficult to create real stakes in this adventure if nobody wants to follow the rules."

"Do you want someone else to be the Tingle Master?" you question. "I could run the game if you want."

"I don't think so," Sarah replies solemnly. "I think I'm just done for a while."

Your friend stands up and gathers her books and dice. At first you think to protest, but you can already tell she's made up her mind.

This may be the session that finally got to Sarah, but it appears she's been considering this exit for a while.

Soon enough, you're the only one left at the table.

In the dim light of the basement, you suddenly feel incredibly lonely. This new world isn't nearly as fun as you'd hoped, and it quickly occurs to you that the best option is heading back into the fantasy realm from which you came.

162

No matter how hard you try, however, you can't seem to return.

"Focus," you tell yourself, closing your eyes tight. "Just remember where you *really* are. You're meditating in a clearing."

Of course, deep down you're not so sure. Are you actually meditating? Or is this new reality the one you truly belong to.

When you open your eyes, you're still sitting at a table in your friend's dimly lit basement.

Regardless of whether or not you belong on this reality, it looks like you're gonna be here for a while.

The future awaits on page 37

Thinking fast, you dive to the side and strike the creature's other eye, rendering him temporarily sightless. Your opponent is now panicking, stumbling about and lashing the air with its enormous reptilian tail. You back away, allowing the dragon a moment to swipe and claw.

"Over here!" you call out, prompting the beast into another fit as it rushes toward your voice.

Of course, by the time the dragon arrives you've already hustled to another side of the cavern. You try this tactic again, yelling at the monster and then watching as it tears into a frenzy and you make your escape.

Soon enough you're in total control, coaxing the dragon into whatever corner of the cave you want. As the pattern continues, you start lashing out with your weapon, a strike here and a strike there as the creature grows battered and bruised.

It's not long before the dragon collapses onto its horde of chocolate milk bottles in defeat, breathing heavy and whimpering as it struggles to keep fighting. The creature attempts to lift itself off the ground, but the vast amount of energy it just wasted is keeping it down.

Your opponent can't see well enough to defend itself, and it's too exhausted to raise its head.

Slay the dragon on page 181
Show mercy on page 99

"Nothing," you offer, then turn back toward the television and settle into your chair a little deeper.

You let out a long sigh, allowing the flickering images to wash over you. While Bad Boys and Buckaroos had once been an escape, your new way to disconnect is by sitting in front of the TV for hours. Honestly, it doesn't matter what's on, just so long as that soft digital hum is flooding your surroundings and washing over your brain like bleach.

Eventually you realize several hours have passed, and the news report has turned into a haunting display of dancing black and white static. You try getting up, but you feel too exhausted to move.

"Zippy?" you call out, your voice echoing through the empty home.

Has it really been a few hours, or has it been longer? You're starting to second guess the time that you've been stuck in this chair, noticing the aging features of your arms and legs. Maybe it's been years.

Hell, maybe it's been decades.

A loud bubbling sound draws your attention back to the television. You watch as black ooze begins to pour forth from the screen, spilling over the edge and running down to the floor in long, dark streaks. As the static hum grows louder, a pool of thick Voidal ooze begins to grow as the base of your entertainment center.

The closer this puddle of black tar creeps toward you, the more you begin to panic, but you now realize you're stuck firmly in place. You can't escape, regardless how desperately you try to free yourself from the confines of this furniture prison.

"Help!" you cry out, the black ooze sputtering forth from the television faster and faster.

The room is beginning to fill with this dark liquid, and as it finally reaches your skin you find yourself truly understanding how much you've missed out on. There's nothing to be found within this shiny black tar, an endless expanse of nothingness that you've created for yourself. After years of denying your own imagination, this is all that's left.

You let out one final scream as the black ooze rises above your head, flooding into your throat.

THE END

"No thanks!" you offer, dismissing the bigfoot and continuing on your way.

You don't get very far.

After a few steps you catch a sharp hiss from between two empty stalls, the abrupt noise halting you in your tracks and drawing your attention.

"Hey!" a figure offers, peaking around the corner and revealing themselves to be a light purple unicorn with a sparkling horn. They're clad in the soft leather outfit that's used by certified sneaks, a crew of outlaw thieves and rogues who live on the edge of society within Billings. "It's really you!"

"Me?" you question, a little confused.

The unicorn nods. "I saw you enter the market and followed you over here. What the hell are you doing?"

"I'm just... trying to find my way," you offer in return. "Do I know you?"

The unicorn shakes his head. "No, but I know you," he offers. "You're part of the prophecy. I'd recognize that face anywhere."

You let out an exhausted sigh. "I've been hearing this prophecy thing a lot today," you admit. "What makes you think yours is the real one?"

"Because it's the prophecy *they don't want you to know about,*" the sneak counters. "Come on, follow me."

With that, the unicorn ducks back behind this empty booth.

Follow the unicorn to page 48
Decline on page 28

166

In one quick movement you reach for your sword, letting go with one hand and swiping at your hilt. Unfortunately, the misplacer beast has used its power to great advantage, and you quickly discover your sword is not where you thought you'd left it.

It's been misplaced.

Now this monster has the upper hand, its snapping jaws creeping closer and closer to your face. You push back against the beast with everything you've got, but the attempt to grab your sword has done you in.

You let out a frantic scream as the creature's jaws close around your head, tearing it clean off.

THE END

You rush toward your blade, sliding across the dirt as the creature lunges over the top of you. Seconds later, your hands find their way around the hilt of your sword, gripping tight as you prepare for the monster's next attack.

The misplacer beast doesn't waste any time, circling back and then snarling loudly as it takes another ferocious leap.

This time you're ready.

Instead of rolling away you hold your ground, positioning your sword directly in front of you and then thrusting up as the beast plunges downward. The creature howls as your weapon sinks deep into its chest cavity with a sickening thud, slicing it clean open and spilling its innards across the dirt in a sticky mess of crimson organs and meat.

The misplacer beast slumps over as you fall back in exhaustion, covered in blood and struggling to catch your breath.

You remain like this for a good while, overwhelmingly thankful for your training. Back at the castle, it was hard to imagine what a real battle would feel like, and at times you felt the rigorous exercises of Lady Norbalo we're a touch overblown.

Now you know the truth.

Suddenly, the moment of silence is broken by a mighty howl that erupts in the distance, this braying song flooding the air and sending a powerful chill down your spine. Soon this cry is joined by another, and another, a whole pack of misplacer beasts announcing their presence.

They must've picked up the scent of their companion's blood, you realize.

Time to move.

You stand up and dust yourself off, then go to grab your sword before finding that the weapon has disappeared. As a final parting gift from this rather irritating beast, your sword is nowhere to be found.

Another howl floats across the golden field, this one even closer than the last. They're headed your way.

Without much time to spare, you're suddenly faced with a horrible choice. Do you stay and search for your misplaced sword, or do you take off running and get a head start on these frightening creatures?

Stay and search page 182
Escape to page 114

"Here's the thing you might not realize about being a bandit," you offer, speaking casually as the coblin weapons remain trained directly at you. "It's a pretty good gig, going around and taking things that aren't yours. Believe me, I understand why you might keep this racket up for a while. The problem is, eventually you're going to steal from the wrong person, someone who's been trained in the magical arts and knows how to defend themselves."

You whip your staff around and swing it like a bat, slamming into three of the sentient vegetables and sending them flying with a surge of blue magical energy. The creatures on the other side of you immediately spring into action, thrusting their spears in your direction, but you're too quick for them.

You dive and roll, then take another swing that knocks one of the creatures so hard it erupts in a flash of blue energy, it's body scattering across the trail as yellow popcorn.

A club strikes you in the back, sending you tumbling, but you quickly regain your composure and lash out at this new attack. You counter well, tearing through yet another opponent with a brilliant flash of blue light.

It's not long before the whole mob has been dispatched, either lying face down in the dirt as blood pools around them, or heated with your magic stuff until they erupt in a shower of popcorn.

You take a deep breath and let it out, centering yourself after an exhausting battle.

You're just about ready to hit the road again when you catch sight of a single coblin scampering off into the woods. They've recovered from their injuries, or they were faking it the whole time. Either way, they're on the run.

Chase the coblin to page 144
Let the coblin escape and keep traveling to page 201

"I'm interested," you finally say.

"Good," the mysterious unicorn retorts. "Then follow me. We've got a long way to go."

The two of us set out on our journey, an epic quest that's just as arduous as my last one because it follows the exact same path. You're headed back to Billings.

Fortunately, you don't have to make as many stops along the way, as all monstrous altercations are avoided. There are a few close calls, but the unicorn uses his skills to guide you in the way of the sneak. Any time a battle appears to be lurking right around the corner, you'll slip into the shadows and find another path around.

As you travel the unicorn explains your true place in this ancient prophecy. There are many interpretations of the "role-player", but according to sneak's guild you fit their description perfectly. As soon as the unicorn spotted you, he knew you were meant to give back to the common folk of this broken world. This is why the king brought you in to accomplish some other red herring quest, a way to keep you busy while the true interpretation of this prophecy is ignored.

Eventually, the wildlands give way to civilization once more. You find yourself in the familiar golden fields that surround billings, trekking over beautiful rolling hills.

You arrived at the looming city wall, this structure of defensive stonework towering over you. Guards patrol across the top, but they're too high to pay much attention to you and your unicorn friend as you creep along in the shadows.

You eventually arrive at a large boulder that pushes against the wall's base. The unicorn gazes up, timing his movements perfectly so that the patrolling guards have their backs turned in unison. Once the coast is clear, he rolls this boulder to the side and reveals a small hole, just big enough for the two of you to slip inside.

The next thing you know, you and your sneak companion are creeping along through the inner workings of Billings, a network of tunnels that weave below this sprawling kingdom.

At one point a loud swarm of giant rats comes skittering past you, causing you to jump in alarm. They're harmless, minding their own business and continuing on their way through the darkness, but this abrupt encounter prompts you to reach for your magic staff and realize it's not there.

In fact, *ALL ITEMS* appear to have disappeared.

"Hey!" you blurt. "What the hell? Where's my stuff?"

The unicorn shrugs. "What? Just because I'm a *sneak* you think I stole your things?"

"Actually, yes," you blurt. "What the hell? I'm here to help you and you take my supplies?"

The unicorn shakes his head, continuing the denial.

"If you don't give my stuff back then I quit," you counter.

The two of you stand in silence for a moment, waiting for the other to break. Finally, the unicorn lets out a long sigh and reaches into his bag, extracting a TURN INTO FROG SCROLL and handing it over to you. "Here. Take this," he offers.

You begrudgingly accept.

"Just don't use it when you're sneaking around, okay?" the unicorn continues. "This isn't a wizard's prophecy, it's a sneak's prophecy. You need to stay in the shadows and not make a big scene. Do you understand?"

"Sure," you reply. "No frog spells while I'm sneaking around."

"Why?" the unicorn continues.

"Because it's a sneak's prophecy," you repeat back before continuing on your way.

Deeper and deeper you venture into this underground labyrinth, until finally your companion pushes away a hanging tarp and reveals a large stone chamber.

There are six figures sitting around a table in this dimly lit room, but when they catch sight of your arrival they all stand and scurry into the shadows. Now, only one entity remains at the central chair, eyeing you skeptically.

The woman is flat a square, a sentient book with the name "The Complete Guide To Sneaks" written in gold letters across her maroon cover. In smaller print, the words "Second edition" can be found, but you have no idea what this could possibly mean. Her corners are worn and scuffed after more adventures than you can imagine.

"Who the hell is this?" the sentient book questions, rolling up a map on the table before her and quickly putting it away.

"You don't recognize them?" your unicorn companion questions.

The living book narrows her eyes, taking you in with slightly closer scrutiny.

Quickly, the unicorn hurries over and gingerly opens her to a page in the middle, peeking within and then glancing back toward you. Your companion does this several times before closing the volume. "Yep, this is the one."

The sentient book's eyes go wide. "The prophecy!" she blurts, then motions for you to come sit across from her.

You do as you're told, pulling out a wooden chair and settling in directly across from this mysterious figure. All the others, including your new unicorn friend, disappear into the shadows.

"I'm Darba, headmaster of the sneaks' guild," the sentient book informs you. "Your face is one that many of our members recognize, written deep within my pages."

You nod along, listening intently.

"While the main tomes of lore have prophecies of their own, I'm what you would call *supplemental material*," the sentient book explains. "I have a prophecy of my own, said to bring joy and peace to this land once again. Unlike the others, this prophecy is not just for those who dwell on the surface."

"What is it?" you question, cutting to the point. "What do you need me to do?"

Darba nods, appreciating your frankness. "You need to steal something from King Rolo," she finally reveals.

You consider her words for a moment, but deep down you already know the answer.

Start your training on page 23

"Fine. I'll come with you," you offer.

The unicorn grins, stepping forward and pulling a sophisticated lockpick from a bag on his belt. He fiddles around with the padlock on your cell for a moment. Seconds later, a hollow, metallic clank erupts forth as the door unlatches and swings open.

"Follow me," the unicorn commands, beckoning you onward as he approaches a nearby torture rack.

The unicorn unfastens a bolt that connects this macabre contraption to the stone wall behind it. He begins to push, eventually revealing a small hole that's just large enough to slip through.

"After you," the unicorn continues, motioning you onward.

You do as you're told, sliding within and finding yourself in a long tunnel. Your unicorn companion follows, pulling the torture device back into position behind him.

The next thing you know you're creeping along through the inner workings of Billings, a network of tunnels that weave through and below this sprawling kingdom.

"Just through here," the unicorn keeps assuring you, but with every new chamber it seems your goal is no closer to arrival.

Deeper and deeper you venture into this underground labyrinth, until finally your companion pushes away a hanging tarp and reveals a large stone chamber.

There are six figures sitting around a table in this dimly lit room, but when they catch sight of your arrival they all stand and scurry into the shadows. Now, only one entity remains at the central chair, eyeing you skeptically.

The woman is flat a square, a sentient book with the name "The Complete Guide To Sneaks" written in gold letters across her maroon cover. In smaller print, the words "Second edition" can be found, but you have no idea what this could possibly mean. Her corners are worn and scuffed after more adventures than you can imagine.

"Who the hell is this?" the sentient book questions, rolling up a map on the table before her and quickly putting it away.

"You don't recognize them?" your unicorn companion questions.

The living book narrows her eyes, taking you in with slightly closer scrutiny.

Quickly, the unicorn hurries over and gingerly opens her to a page in the middle, peeking within and then glancing back toward you. Your companion does this several times before closing the volume. "Yep, this is the one."

The sentient book's eyes go wide. "The prophecy!" she blurts, then motions for you to come sit across from her.

You do as you're told, pulling out a wooden chair and settling in directly across from this mysterious figure. All the others, including your new unicorn friend, disappear into the shadows.

"I'm Darba, headmaster of the sneaks' guild," the sentient book informs you. "Your face is one that many of our members recognize, written deep within my pages."

You nod along, listening intently.

"While the main tomes of lore have prophecies of their own, I'm what you would call *supplemental material*," the sentient book explains. "I have a prophecy of my own, said to bring joy and peace to this land once again. Unlike the others, this prophecy is not just for those who dwell on the surface."

"What is it?" you question, cutting to the point. "What do you need me to do?"

Darba nods, appreciating your frankness. "You need to steal something from King Rolo," she finally reveals.

Your heart skips a beat, and the living book immediately notices your hesitance.

"Please understand, we'll be forced to kill you if you say no," she continues "The secrets of the sneaks' guild cannot leave this chamber."

Accept the mission on page 23
Decline the mission on page 224

174

As much as you appreciate Amanda saving your life, this is a solo mission. Who knows the technicalities of fulfilling this prophecy? Does it count if you travel with a partner?

"I'm sorry," you finally offer. "I think I need to do this on my own."

The bumblebeeholder takes a moment to accept the news, then finally offers a nod of understanding. "Okay then," she replies. "Good luck out there."

With that, the creature buzzes along and leaves you to stand alone in the deep dark forest.

You finish dusting yourself off and continue on your way.

Resume the journey on page 17

You give up immediately, realizing there's no way out of this pickle and admitting defeat gracefully. The guards surround you, stripping away *ALL ITEMS* and pushing you roughly into the jail cell that once held this despondent twenty-sided die.

"The punishment for traitors is death," the living die snarls as he watches from a new side of the bars. "So much for the prophecy."

With that, the mob of imposing guards leaves you to yourself, exiting the dungeon and locking the thick iron door behind them.

As the minutes stretch into hours the silence becomes overwhelming, nothing but a strange aural emptiness wrapping itself around you. Every so often the faint sounds of some distant torture session will tickle your ears, but otherwise the dungeon retains a bizarre stillness that you rarely find in the outside world.

You realize the question's not *if* you'll be executed for your crime, but when, and this haunting truth seems to linger behind every thought that works its way through your mind. Confronting your own mortality is a tall order, especially when you've found yourself with a swiftly approaching expiration date.

"Frightening to look death in the face, isn't it?" comes an unexpected voice from the shadows.

You sit up abruptly in your cot, staring out into the darkness as a figure begins to emerge. You see a unicorn in thieves' gear on the other side of the bars, the mysterious visitor grinning with an expression of bemused empathy.

"I've been there before, many times," the unicorn offers. "Only difference is that *I'm* not the subject of a world changing prophecy. You are."

"The prophecy is wrong," you retort. "That's how I ended up here."

"Maybe that's because you're looking at the *wrong prophecy,*" the unicorn counters. "I'll free you from this cage if you're willing to come with me."

As nice as the offer sounds, there's part of you that wonders if this is yet another test. Maybe the *real* way to regain your freedom is to simply accept the hand you're dealt.

Besides, even if this isn't another trial from King Rolo, all is not lost. You still might be able to talk some sense into your captors before the execution arrives.

"What do you say?" the unicorn questions, waiting for your response.

Go with the unicorn on page 172
Decline on page 73

Your sympathy for this living die finally bubbles up and boils over, flooding you with mercy as you approach the jail cell. You pull out your dungeon key, glancing both ways before finally slipping it into the lock and turning it sharply.

The sentient die is free.

"Thank you," the living object before you states as you back away from the bars.

Suddenly, however, his expression changes from one of deep sincerity to profound anger. The living die reaches behind him and withdraws an enormous glistening blade, then kicks the cell door open with a loud clatter.

"Guards!" the former prisoner calls out gruffly. "They've failed the test! King Rolo cannot trust this traitor!"

Heavy footsteps ring out as the sentient twenty-sided die begins to advance toward you, weapon drawn.

There are too many of them to fight, so your options are limited. Either turn yourself in or make a run for it.

Run away to page 67
Turn yourself in on page 175

"Alright," you reply. "I'll arm wrestle you."

You wade into the trash pile, meeting the troll halfway. The large green creature is positioned behind a small table, and you sit down across from him.

There's no question this slimy green monster is much larger than you are, an imposing physical presence by any measure. However, just because the troll is large, it doesn't mean he's strong.

Arm wrestling is more than just a contest of bodily might, it's also a test of willpower and mental resolve. You've seen plenty of tavern arguments settled over an unbalanced match where the much smaller contestant ended up victorious, and it's always because they brough more heart to the battle.

The troll places his arm on the table before you, taking his position, but you hesitate before grabbing onto the creature's massive hand.

You need to pump yourself up, but there are several methods of accomplishing this task.

On one hand, it would be easy enough to draw on the anger you feel toward this troll, to focus on the horrible messages he's been sending out and the negativity he's brought upon this kingdom. It's frustrating to think about, and that frustration seems like the perfect fuel for this particular contest.

There is, however, another way. While it's easy to harness the power of anger in a physical test, the power of love can be just as potent. There's something about this troll that's profoundly sad, a creature who allowed his negativity to grow and mutate until it overwhelmed him completely. Maybe the real solution is to draw from the love that you feel for your life, for this adventure, and even for the troll in some strange nebulous way.

Use the power of anger on page 103
Use the power of love on page 179

While there's certainly a time and place for healthy anger, you decide to draw on the power of love to pump yourself up.

You focus this positive energy, then reach out and take the troll's hand in yours. The two of you stare at one another across the table, eyes locked as the countdown begins.

"Three, two, one," you say in unison.

Suddenly, the two of you are pushing hard against one another, your palms wobbling back and forth as you struggle to force the troll down. His size is a huge advantage, but your predictions about the creature's actual strength we're dead on.

Still, arm wrestling a troll is no easy task, and you feel your muscles quickly beginning to weaken. You find yourself slipping, the strength draining out of your body as fatigue overwhelms you.

It's time to turn on the afterburners.

You close your eyes, allowing love to overwhelm you. Almost instantly, the might within your hand alters course. You can feel your power growing, the tides of battle shifting as you slowly push back against the troll.

Seconds later, you're slamming his hand down against the table. You are victorious.

"Ah ha!" you shout excitedly, erupting from your seat. "You're out of here!"

The troll sighs and nods, slowly climbing to his feet as food remnants and various discarded wrappers roll off his body. "Okay," he sighs.

"No more messages tied to rats either," you continue. "If you don't want this dagger in you, then you need to lay low. They've gotta think you're dead."

The troll nods again, gathering some of his things as he prepares to leave.

"Hey!" you snap, drawing his attention. "Don't make me come find you."

The troll reaches up and grabs a tuft of his own stringy black hair, yanking hard and pulling it from his head in an enormous patch. "Here," he offers. "Evidence you stuck me with that dagger of yours."

He hands over the hair, then turns and waddles off onto the darkness.

180

You don't expect to ever see this troll again.

The second the troll leaves you turn and make your way back up to the world above. You don't wanna stay in this putrid chamber one second longer than you have to, and you're ready to continue your training with Lady Norbalo.

Return victorious on page 33

You triumphantly approach the creature, ready to shove your weapon deep into one of its wounded eyes and deliver the final blow. Before you get a chance, however, the dragon snaps it's head forward in a sudden, violent burst.

Yes, the creature is exhausted, but they're also a devious opponent who knows how to draw you in. The dragon saved just enough energy to deliver a devastating bite, and now it's open jaws are headed right for you.

If you have the staff turn to page 121
If you don't have the staff turn to page 133

182

Realizing you'll need a weapon as you continue on your journey, you decide to take your chances with a quick search of the area. You immediately spring into action, hunting for the missing sword, but with every passing second the howls of this ravenous misplacer beast pack grow louder and louder.

Thanks to the magical powers of these strange creatures, your sword could be anywhere, but you quickly narrow your search down to two distinct locations.

The first potential option is that your weapon has disappeared under the fresh corpse right next to you, resting somewhere beneath the beast's thick fur. Otherwise, a tangled root system under the nearby tree might hold the key to your missing sword.

To search the tree turn to page 199
To search the creature's body turn to page 105

You see the opening and you take it. Holding your breath and gripping your weapon tight, you begin to make your way up to the sleeping dragon, careful not to disturb the piles of chocolate milk bottles as you go. Your movements are slow and measured, your eyes trained on the ferocious beast.

Closer and closer you draw, the fear within you suddenly joined by yet another distinct emotion: pride. You realize suddenly that you're about to fulfill the prophecy and save the kingdom, a true hero who saw their journey through from beginning to end.

And to think, it all comes down to a final battle where your opponent is drifting in dreamland, fast asleep and unable to defend themselves. It seems a little anticlimactic, to be honest.

You're right next to the dragon's face now, struggling to determine the most effective death blow when suddenly the creature's eyes fly open and a smile erupts across his once stoic visage.

You can see in the dragon's jet black eyes that he's not at all startled. He's been fully aware of your presence this whole time, just begging for you to draw a little closer.

Now you're right where he wants you.

Before you have a chance to deliver your attack the massive beast opens its mouth and spews forth a tidal wave of sticky black tar, the toxic mess sweeping you away and covering your body completely. You open your mouth to scream but the ooze quickly fills you up, wrapping you in its cold, cosmic embrace.

You make a brief attempt to swim to the surface, but you quickly realize there's no salvation to be found. Endless nothingness lies in every direction, a plane of all that cannot be.

The very thought of this pushes you into a state of utter madness, your mind struggling to understand what's happening to the world around you as existence itself collapses like the center of a dying black hole.

The Void consumes you.

THE END

184

You decide to approach your boss first, understanding the risks but also recognizing he'd make a great addition to the game.

Your heart pumping, you stand up from your cubicle and make your way through the office like it's some dangerous, fantasy-realm cavern. Your bosses office looms before you, the dragon's den from which there may be no turning back.

You knock on the door.

"Come in!" a deep voice calls out from the other side.

The second you push into Krimble's lair you realize this was a terrible idea. He looks flustered and anxious, an assortment of papers spread across his desk in haphazard piles. Krimble barely glances up at you as his eyes dart from report to report, deeply focused.

"Yeah, what?" he blurts.

"Oh," you stammer. "I was just wondering... I have this fantasy game I used to play and I was thinking about starting up again. Have you ever tried Bad Boys and Buckaroos."

Finally, Krimble stops what he's doing and looks up at you in exasperated frustration. You finally have his full attention, but it's certainly not for the right reason.

"Are you kidding me?" he snarls.

"Sorry," is all you can think to say.

Krimble returns his attention to the paperwork on his desk. "Don't let me catch you talking about that again or you're fired. Get back to work."

Without another word you turn and leave Krimble's office, slinking back to your cubicle in defeat. You catch Ashley's gaze as you go, but the two of you quickly avert your eyes. Maybe this wasn't such a good idea after all.

By the time you've collapsed back into your chair, the excitement of a potential game has worn off completely. Your memories of a fantasy world have faded away, replaced by the anxiety of some upcoming report deadline.

THE END

There's something about this riddle that seems vaguely familiar, the answer floating through the back of your mind like some subconscious connection to a distant timeline. You close your eyes for a moment, drawing on the knowledge of your other self.

Your mind is racing, calculating various ways of looking at this problem and then finally settling on your answer.

You open your eyes and press the button marked 'miss'.

There's a sharp clang, followed by a rapid ticking sound from deep within the safe. You freeze in place, not sure if these noises are a sign of utter disaster or a job well done.

You don't have to wait long to find out.

The safe door pops open, swinging wide to reveal a horde of gold bars and rare jewels. The assortment is so sparkling and brilliant that it feels as though the whole closet is lighting up around you, illuminating your face as you scoop the treasure into your bag.

It quickly becomes apparent that this safe is much larger than you expected. From the outside, it's construction is simple enough, but the space itself pushes deeper and deeper into the stone wall. The safe extends so far that, by the end, you're actually crawling within this oblong compartment to get all the gold out, and *even then* it just keeps coming.

Before long, you realize this safe is just as magical as the arcane bag that you hold in your hands. Just when you think you've found the end of the treasure, more seems to appear.

Finally, after what seems like forever, you've managed to scoop out every last drop of King Rolo's horde.

Your magic bag gets the job done. It's fully loaded, yet shows no sign of overstuffing as it hangs daintily from your belt.

The treasure now in tow, you creep out of the kings closet, through his chambers, and into the hallway. Here you discover the guard dog is still happily munching away at his plate of spaghetti, licking up the last of the sauce but still distracted enough to offer little by way of acknowledgement.

You slither through the shadows, continuing silently through the castle and eventually disappearing into the night from which you came.

Carry out the rest of the plan on page 82

186

"Dragon!" you bellow, your voice echoing through the cavern and flooding the room with depth and power. "I'm here to fight, so face me with honor!"

The massive creature's jet black eyes fly open as you say this, and a mischievous smile flickers across his enormous reptilian face. You realize now he was only feigning sleep, coaxing you toward his mouth in hopes of delivering some devastating sneak attack.

The dragon lets out a horrific gurgling screech and belches forth a cascade of Voidal tar, the dark ooze spewing forth as you dive out of the way. You roll to safety behind a thick rocky pillar, the toxic liquid just missing you as it splashes against the back wall.

Realizing this attack has been unsuccessful, the dragon whips its powerful tail in your direction, slicing the pillar in half. You duck just in time for this attack sails directly over your head, showered in dust and rocks as you hurry on to another section of rocky cover.

You wait here for a moment, analyzing the beast's movements before finally rushing out and delivering some attacks of your own. You strike the dragon several times, but quickly discover your weapons are ineffective against the armor-like scales that cover his enormous body.

You need to focus your fire, to concentrate on a specific and vulnerable section of the dragon's frame.

Attack the dragon's belly on page 193
Attack the dragon's eye on page 25
Attack the dragon's heart on page 88

You shake your head. "It was lost in my battle with the troll. That blade is long gone."

"Very well then," the unicorn replies. "You needed something fit for a warrior anyway."

Lady Norbalo reaches behind her and pulls forth a beautifully crafted STEEL SWORD. She hands it over to you.

"Fashioned by the finest blacksmith in Billings," the unicorn continues. "This blade should guide you well."

While a longer graduation ceremony might be nice, there's little time to waste now that your training is completed. Every day the darkness grows, and now it's up to you to stop it.

Soon enough, you're heading out through the city gates, finding yourself in the beautiful rolling fields of yellow grass that surround Billings. The sight is absolutely majestic, and although you've taken in this landscape plenty of times before, you can't help but give this glorious golden vision some extra weight within your mind. The adventure that lies ahead is a dangerous one, and there's a good chance you may never see these fields again.

According to Lady Norbalo the dragon is located due North, which means you won't have the comfort of a dirt road for the majority of your trek. You'll be stuck walking directly through the rolling grass for quite some time.

Without a moment's hesitation, you head off into the open fields, cutting a straight line across these wide open plains.

The city grows smaller behind you as the sun creeps its way across the sky. You walk for hours, then gradually come to rest under the shade of an old gnarled tree that has sprung up as a singular landmark across this vacant landscape. Out here, the grass is even taller than before, grown so high that you can barely see over the top of it.

Exhausted from the morning hike, you sit down on one of the tree's large roots, reaching back and opening your traveler's pack. You're searching for the lunch you brought along, but it quickly becomes apparent your food has been misplaced.

You could've sworn you packed it, you think to yourself, a certainty that's so overwhelming it causes a spark of alarm to ignite within you.

There's no way you could've *naturally* misplaced your lunch.

188

Suddenly, an enormous misplacer beast leaps at you from the tall grass.

Dodge to the left on page 109
Dodge to the left on page 109
Dodge to the right on page 200

"I accept," you finally reply with a nod.

The bigfoot smiles. "Very good. Your training begins now."

The next month is spent in hardcore arcane preparation, Grimble the Grey taking you through a wizardly masterclass unlike anything you've ever experienced. All the while, your bigfoot teacher is blown away by just how quickly the magical energy flows through you. There are several lessons that ordinarily take *years* to understand, yet within a week or so you're taking control any harnessing this energy.

Of course, you're still nowhere near the level of Grimble himself, but that's not the point. Your real lessons will begin when you set out for Storb's dark tower at the edge of the world.

Eventually, the day arrives when Grimble raises his hand and tells you to stop.

You're deep in your studies, pouring over some ancient tome of magical lore when the bigfoot halts you abruptly.

"It's time," Grimble says. "The power of The Void grows stronger every day. If you don't set out on your quest soon then Count Storb will be too powerful."

You stand up from your desk and approach the bigfoot wizard. He's holding an assortment of magical tools, and he hands them over to you in a state of deep reverence.

The first item you receive is a BLUE STAFF. This weapon is used as a conduit for your arcane powers, capable of focusing your magical energy while attacking or defending in combat. It is a piece of beautifully carved wood, with arcs of turquoise lightening the course through it as you channel your abilities.

Next, you receive two scrolls. These parchments contain detailed magical instructions, which can be read aloud to produce incredible effects. Unfortunately, after a scroll is read the energy is spent and it will turn to dust, so these items must be reserved for the right occasion.

The first scroll is a WEB SCROLL. This item allows you to catch a large group in a web of magical energy, slowing them down or possibly stopping them entirely.

The second scroll is a TURN INTO FROG SCROLL, which will cause any single target to, unsurprisingly, turn into a frog. If you decide to refrain from slaying the evil sorcerer outright, turning him into a frog is another option.

190

As a final gift, Grimble the Grey provides you with a map to Count Storb's tower at the edge of the world. This vile building is located in the middle of a dark swamp, and it'll take quite a bit of travel through dangerous wildlands to get there.

Time is limited, so you say your goodbyes and head out immediately.

Hit the road on page 35

It gradually occurs to you the spaghetti is only necessary if you encounter this notorious guard dog, but if you avoid him entirely then you'll be just fine. By heading into the kitchen and stealing food during someone's apparent night shift, you're putting yourself in a risky situation that could very well be needless.

Now that you're a highly trained member of the sneak's guild, you have faith in a more direct path. You've got this.

You pull back, slinking away from the kitchen and returning to the castle's main foyer. Here, you begin to creep your way up the large staircase in utter silence. You're like a ghost, a phantom of the night who will avoid even the most scrutinizing detection efforts.

Once reaching the upper landing, you begin to make your way down a series of long, twisting hallways.

Sneak along to page 55

You muster all the strength you possibly can, focusing your energy as you push this monstrous canine up and away from your body. It appears all of your training has paid off, because you're actually making some headway, but before you get a chance to toss this ferocious misplacer beast to the side it lashes out a tentacle and slices open your arm with an array of sharp barbs.

The wound isn't deep, but it's more than enough to make you cry out in shock and lose your focus. You pull back and the monster uses this moment to strike, snapping its jaws down right next to the space your head used to occupy. Fortunately, you saw this move coming from a mile away and have managed to roll out from under the misplacer beast.

You've only got a few seconds to collect yourself and plan your next move as the creature turns and prepares another lunge. In this time, however, you catch sight of your misplaced sword. It's leaning against the base of the nearby tree, humming with magical energy and just wanting to join the fray.

Of course, as this enormous monster prepares its next attack you're made keenly aware it might be wiser to turn and run.

This tall grass could be the key to your escape.

Run to page 143
Grab your sword and fight on page 211

You decide to go for the dragon's soft underbelly, rushing toward the creature and courageously swinging away.

Your weapon strikes its target again and again with little effect, but still you push onward, struggling to make any headway in your assault on this massive beast.

You duck and dodge as the dragon swipes with its razor sharp claws, gradually noticing its movements are faltering.

If you have the steel sword or the staff turn to page 198
If you have the blue sword or the orange sword turn to page 75

You're still not convinced this path is for you, and as the unicorn slinks away you can't help but think this is just another journey where you'll be taking orders and doing someone else's dirty work.

"I'm good," you call over. "No thanks."

The sneaking unicorn stops and turns back to you. "Wait, really?" he calls out from his place in the golden grass.

"Yeah," you reply.

There's a moment of hesitation before the unicorn speaks again, the mysterious rogue struggling to collect his thoughts. "So... are you just going to turn down every storyline that comes your way?"

"I guess so," you reply.

The unicorn waits a little longer, then finally shrugs and disappears into the field.

You continue down the road a few more hours, your path gradually growing more and more unkept and wild. Previously, you'd notice a few carts or travelers on horseback along the way, but now they've become few and far between. Soon enough, they've disappeared completely, leaving you all alone in this endless expanse.

You realize now you've crossed over the edge of civilization, entering the wildlands where the rule of order gives way to the reign of monsters.

The reality of your situation is exemplified when you notice something creeping through the grass to your right. It's large and traveling along next to you, some massive, muscular creature that stalks you in complete silence.

You try your best to remain calm, but it quickly dawns on you how woefully unprepared you are for this situation. You've received no training in combat or magic, and you have no weapons to defend yourself.

Slowly, you reach down and grab a large rock on the side of the road, trying your best to seem casual in your movements. You don't look directly at your pursuer, but you keep close watch on this shadowy figure from the corner of your eye.

A low, rumbling growl begins to emit from your stalker, a signal that it's ready to strike. The next thing you know, a giant monster is leaping from the grass, it's massive jaws opening wide as it lunges toward you.

You recognize this creature immediately.

Your attacker is a misplacer beast, an enormous canine species with jet black fur and sharp, gnashing teeth. It stands on four muscular legs and is approximately eight feet long, but the thing that's truly frightening about this ferocious creature are the two long tentacles that rise from either shoulder blade. These slithering appendages are incredibly powerful, used to slash and whip their prey, and feature spiked pads at the end of their fur-covered length.

Of course, this fearsome predator is more than just its physical presence. All misplacer beasts are humming with magical energy, an unseen force that constantly swirls around them and causes their opponents to misplace things.

This effect couldn't be more apparent as you go to bash the creature with your sharp rock and realize this makeshift weapon has disappeared from your grip. It's been misplaced.

Before you have a chance to readjust, the monster is upon you, biting down with its sharp jaws and tearing you open for its next meal.

THE END

Drawn to the swirling red and white design, you finally decide to go with Spaghetti For Life.

"That one," you offer, tapping on the glass.

Jorlin nods and the cashier reaches in to extract your chosen ticket, handing it over as Jorlin pays.

Soon enough, the two of you are strolling back to the house as your friend sips away at his cold chocolate milk. His mood is already starting to improve, and for a moment you consider just forgetting about the lottery card in an effort to ride this wave of good vibes.

Before you have a chance, however, your friend pulls out a coin and flashes you his ticket. "Let's see if tonight's our lucky night," he offers, finishing his milk and tossing it into a trash can. Jorlin approaches a nearby wall and presses his ticket against it, using the hard surface as he scratches away at a little cartoon meatball.

Slowly, various numbers are revealed, but the longer Jorlin spends scraping away at this tiny card, the more his mood begins to shift back toward anger and frustration.

Eventually, he reaches the final meatball and reveals a complete loss. There are no matches.

"Well... damn," is all Jorlin can think to say.

"It's just a game," you offer.

Your friend nods, smiling as the two of you continue on your way, but despite Jorlin's feigned expression you can tell something's not right with him. Jorlin's mind is racing now, and the general unease is creeping its way through him no matter how hard he tries to push it away.

Soon enough, the two of you are making your way up the front steps and pushing through the door. From here it's a straight shot down the hallway, and you can see Lorbo is sitting exactly where he was before, perched on the back porch as he sips away at a cool glass of chocolate milk.

You approach your friend, hoping to mediate an even-keeled conversation.

"Hey man," you offer. "We should have a talk."

"I'm listening," Lorbo retorts, his gaze fixed across the back yard.

"You've gotta stop thinking about the rules," Jorlin blurts with belligerent aggression. "We don't *need* rules to play. The whole point is to have fun."

Not off to a good start.

"You ever think that someone else might *enjoy* structure?' Lorbo counter.

"That's ridiculous," Jorlin snaps.

You try interjecting a point about the importance of compromise, but your attempt is immediately steamrolled by Lorbo.

"You're a dick," Lorbo states loudly, still staring off into the darkness of his back yard as he takes a long, slow sip of his chocolate milk.

"Do you even want to play?" Jorlin cries out, throwing his hands up. "Would you rather just look at a spreadsheet of combat stats?"

Finally, Lorbo turns to face us, a deep intensity in his gaze that looks like a mixture of frustration and sorrow. "Maybe we shouldn't have either," he states flatly. "I think you guys should leave."

We stand motionless for a moment, slowly recognizing the final bridge has been crossed. There's no turning back now.

"The group is finished?" you question.

"I think so," Lorbo replies.

Jorlin and you exchange solemn glances, then head back inside to collect your things.

The future awaits on page 37

198

Despite your training, the weapon in your hands is simply not enough to stop this powerful, monstrous force. You can see the dragon weakening slightly, but it still has more than enough energy to snap its neck forward and slice you clean in half with a well-placed bite.

As the beast tosses your lower half into the air and gobbles it down, you gaze up at the ceiling of the cavern. Your vision is fading, but at least you're dying in the heat of battle and not drifting off into the endless cosmic Void that has so thoroughly destroyed this land.

The prophecy was not fulfilled, but you don't have time to worry about that any longer.

You lay back in the pile of chocolate milk bottles and close your eyes, accepting your fate as a tragic hero.

THE END

Thinking fast, you decide to search around in the tree's twisted root system. You rush over and begin frantically reaching into the hidden spaces that make up this strange network, desperately yearning for your hand to find itself wrapped around a familiar hilt.

You search your way around the base of the tree, but by the time you've done a complete circle you recognize a new presence in this small clearing. You glace up to see five misplacer beasts slinking out from within the tall grass, their tentacles whipping the air and their mouths watering with anticipation.

Even with a weapon to defend yourself, this is not a fight you could win. As an unarmed warrior, you might as well be served up on a platter next to a sprig of parsley.

As the misplacer beasts descend upon you, your screams echo out across the vast plains. They don't last long.

THE END

200

You leap to the right and narrowly avoid this snarling, ferocious misplacer beast.

The creature is an enormous canine with jet black fur and sharp, gnashing teeth. It stands on four muscular legs and is approximately eight feet long, but the thing that's truly frightening about this ferocious creature are the two long tentacles that rise from either shoulder blade. These slithering appendages are incredibly powerful, used to slash and whip their prey, and feature spiked pads at the end of their fur-covered length.

Of course, this fearsome predator is more than just its physical presence. All misplacer beasts are humming with magical energy, an unseen force that constantly swirls around them and causes their opponents to misplace things.

It goes without saying that you find yourself empty handed as you reach back for your weapon, the sheathe completely empty. Somehow your sword has been misplaced.

It takes no more than a second to catch sight of your lost blade resting quietly against the nearby tree, but with this hungry misplacer beast ready for its second pounce, it might be wiser to turn and run.

This tall grass could be the key to your escape.

Run to page 143
Grab your blade and fight on page 167

After a moment of internal debate you finally decide this runaway coblin just isn't worth the time or effort. Instead of chasing them down, you let the sentient vegetable scamper off into the woods and continue on your way.

With a first battle now under your belt, you feel a bit more confident in your shoes as an adventurer. Being the one to fulfill some ancient prophecy is a tall order, but with every step along this quest you find yourself becoming more and more comfortable in the role.

You travel for ten more minutes, your head full of grandiose thoughts of the future until, suddenly, another coblin steps onto the path directly before you.

You stop in your tracks, staring at this bold creature in utter confusion and then eventually recognizing him as the sentient corn you allowed to escape just moments earlier.

"You should've stayed gone," you offer. "I was doing you a favor by not hunting you down."

"You!" the coblin retorts, pointing and shouting angrily.

You shake your head. "Didn't you see what I did to all your friends? Now there's only one of you, and you don't even have a spear anymore!"

The corn on the cob points again. "Alone!" he cries.

"I'm alone?" you retort with a laugh. "No, *you're* alone."

The coblin shakes his head.

Suddenly, more and more of the creatures begin to emerge from the woods, stepping out from their hiding places with smug looks plastered across their vegetable faces.

It appears this final coblin ran off and found some reinforcements, and while the first group of bandits provided only a handful of attackers to contend with, you're now surrounded by forty or so of the angry creatures.

Earlier they simply wanted to rob you, but now they have an ax to grind.

"I'll give you whatever you want!" you suddenly blurt, scrambling to open up your bag.

Before you get the chance the sentient corns charge you, hoisting their spears and impaling your body from every angle.

THE END

202

In one quick movement you reach for your sword, letting go with one hand and swiping at the hilt in your sheathe. Unfortunately, the misplacer beast has used its power to great advantage, and you quickly discover your sword is not where you thought you'd left it.

Now the monster on top of you has the upper hand, it's snapping jaws creeping closer and closer to your face.

In a moment of inspiration, however, you decide to search for your sword in the last place you'd ever look. With your final crumbs of strength, you use your free hand to reach behind the massive canine's ear, discovering this is exactly where your sword was misplaced.

The creature opens wide to bite your head, but before it can chomp down you thrust your magic sword up into the belly of the misplacer beast. Your opponent immediately seizes up as pain and discomfort surge through it, relaxing enough that you can easily push this monster to the side.

You withdraw your sword and watch as the creature fades away, its tenacles twitching for a moment before finally coming to rest in the blood soaked dirt. You wipe the viscera from your blade, taking a moment to collect yourself.

Soon enough, you're resuming your journey.

Your quest continues on page 76

You consider this for a moment, weighing the question in your mind.

While you can understand the arguments on either side, it feels like the best way to have a tabletop role-playing session everyone enjoys is to honor both aspects of the game. Having fun is obviously very important, but that's only possible with some respect for rules and structure. It's about finding a balance between the two.

"Both," you finally confirm. "There's no right or wrong way to play, so it's perfectly reasonable for players to enjoy different aspects of the game. The key is in finding a way for everyone to get what they're looking for, and that means providing equal parts structure and fun."

Sarah nods, her expression warming as she realizes she's not alone in her opinion. As the Tingle Master, finding this kind of balance falls mostly on her shoulders, and this can amount to *a lot* of work. She seems deeply thankful to learn that you're on her side.

"I wish Jorlin and Lorbo could realize that, too," Sarah offers.

You nod. "I'll go talk to them. If we're gonna work together in the *fantasy world*, then we've also gotta work together out here."

You stand and head up the stairs, exiting the dimly lit basement and finding yourself on the first floor of Lorbo's modest home. You notice Lorbo to your right, his back to you as he sits on the porch and sips from a tall glass of chocolate milk. He's gazing out into the dark evening, deep in thought.

To your left, you barely catch a glimpse of Jorlin as he makes his way up the street, angrily storming away from the house.

Follow Jorlin to page 210
Talk to Lorbo on page 74

You decide to adjust your aim the slightest bit to the right, recognizing that your throws usually have a hook to them. You envision the path of the rock in your hand, picture the way it will look and feel as it travels through the air in a clean, even arc and strikes your target.

You take a deep breath, then throw.

Unfortunately, your initial adjustment was slightly off, and although your trajectory *does* hook a bit, it's not nearly enough to make up for the difference in your aim.

Your rock sails past the tree and lands in the shrubbery nearby.

"Welp, guess that's that," Lorbo states solemnly.

Suddenly, the door opens behind you and Jorlin steps onto the porch. "Ready to talk?" he questions.

Lorbo laughs. "If you're ready to apologize."

"I mean... not really," Jorlin counters.

You interject quickly, hoping to head this conversation off at the pass. "Hey! Can't we just find a middle ground here?"

Lorbo glances over at you, confused, then stands up and takes an aggressive stance. "Middle ground?" he blurts. "There's no reasoning with Jorlin."

Jorlin just shakes his head with disappointment. "So I'm the one who can't find a middle ground? You really think *I'm* the problem?"

He's directing his question at you for some reason, but Jorlin jumps in to answer. "Yeah, you're the problem," he shouts, raising his voice to a previously uncharted volume. "Where the hell do you get off telling me the rules don't matter in my own house?"

"It's *our* game!" Lorbo counters.

"Not anymore," comes a voice from behind you.

The group turns to see Sarah standing in the doorway. She looks utterly exhausted, shaking her head from side to side in disappointment as she watches the three of you fight like paladins and rogues.

"This is too much," Sarah continues. "It's just not fun if everyone's gonna be like this. Bad Boys and Buckaroos is about *escaping* the problems of the real world, not starting new ones."

Your first instinct is to immediately contradict her, to push for your group to stay together and keep playing like you always have, but for some reason you just can't get my mouth to form the words.

Maybe she's right.

"Guess that's the end, then," Lorbo finally replies. "You all should pack up and head home."

The future awaits on page 37

"Listen, I totally agree with you," you finally admit. "Lorbo's being a jerk."

"Right?" Jorlin cries out, throwing his hands in the air. "Who the hell cares about the rules when you're having a good time? That's the whole point isn't it?"

You'd been trying your best to stay partial on the matter, but Jorlin's enthusiasm strikes a chord deep within you. You have to admit, he's making a lot of sense.

You begin to nod along as Jorlin rants away, letting all the frustration out of his system like the air of some toxic balloon. He takes you through a series of peaks and valleys, alternating between sadness and anger as this emotional diatribe spills forth and makes its way across your ears.

Your head begins to nod along, involuntarily bobbing up and down with every consecutive good point that Jorlin makes. When he finally wraps it up, you've been fully convinced.

"Listen, you're a hundred percent correct with all this, but we still need to keep the group together," you explain. "Let's go back and lay it out for Lorbo. Maybe we can change his mind."

Jorlin agrees and soon enough the two of you are headed back to the house, making your way up the front steps and pushing through the door. From here it's a straight shot down to hallway, and you can see Lorbo is sitting exactly where he was before, perched on the back porch as he sips away at a cold glass of chocolate milk.

You approach your friend.

"Hey man," you offer. "We should have a talk."

"I'm listening," Lorbo retorts, his gaze fixed across the back yard.

"You've gotta stop thinking so much about the rules," Jorlin blurts. "We don't need rules to play. The whole point is to have fun."

"You ever consider that someone might *enjoy* structure?' Lorbo counter.

"That's ridiculous," Jorlin snaps.

You suddenly realize this is on the verge of getting way out of hand. Coming in hot and trying to steamroll through Lorbo's preferences was clearly not the best approach, as least if you goal is holding the group together.

"You're a dick," Lorbo offers, still staring off into the darkness of his back yard as he takes a long, slow sip of his chocolate milk.

"Do you even *want* to play?" Jorlin cries out, throwing his hands up. "Would you rather just look at a spreadsheet of combat stats?"

Finally, Lorbo turns to face us, a deep intensity in his gaze that looks like a mixture of frustration and sorrow. "Maybe we shouldn't have either," he states flatly. "I think you guys should leave."

We stand motionless for a moment, slowly recognizing the final bridge has been crossed. There's no turning back now.

"The group is finished?" you question.

"I think so," Lorbo replies.

Jorlin and you exchange solemn glances, then head back inside to collect your things.

The future awaits on page 37

As your sense of danger grows you find yourself breaking into a run. After all, sometimes the only way out is through. You begin to sprint down the trail, glancing over your shoulder as the bushes continue to quake and move.

Suddenly, a sharp screeching cry erupts through the air, the unmistakable call of a coblin hunting party.

Coblins are short, sentient corn on the cob's, a ruthless species of living object who patrol these areas as small war bands. They are carnivores, and enjoy the taste of human flesh on occasion. Most of these roadside assaults are strictly for profit, small time bandit raids where they steal your items and take off into the forest.

Unfortunately, running away from the coblins has triggered their innate passion for the hunt. If they see something trying to flee, they'll chase it, and at this crossroad you're more likely to end up a meal than the victim of theft.

A thrown spear suddenly hits the dirt next to you, narrowly missing your heels by a few feet. Your eyes go wide in alarm as you struggle to run even faster, but before you get the chance a second spear impales you through the back.

You collapse to the ground, the weapon driven clean through your body and holding you in place. Your vision fading, you look up to see a mob of coblins surrounding you, the living vegetables licking their lips with hungry anticipation.

THE END

While Chuck's offer is certainly an interesting one, you still don't know if the true buckaroo path is right for you. There's a wide open world of adventure out there, and locking yourself into a lane of stoic personal exploration isn't quite what you're looking for.

"I don't know if that's the best journey for me," you finally admit.

Chuck nods. "That's okay, buckaroo. There are all kinds of trots that prove love is real, you'll find one that fits your unique way."

With that, the mysterious figure hops down from his place on the stone wall and makes his way out into the field, slowly disappearing from sight as he fades into the golden grass.

You turn to continue on your journey, but you don't get very far. After a few steps you hear a sharp hiss from behind the crumbling stone wall, the sound halting you in your tracks and drawing your attention.

"Hey!" the figure cuts in, peaking up over the ledge and revealing themselves to be a light purple unicorn with a sparkling horn. They're clad in the soft leather outfit that's used by certified sneaks, a crew of outlaw thieves and rogues who live on the edge of society within Billings. "It's really you!"

"Me?" you question, a little confused.

The unicorn nods. "I saw you back in the city and followed you out here. What the hell are you doing?"

"I'm just... trying to find my way," you offer in return. "Do I know you?"

The unicorn shakes their head. "No, but I know you," he offers. "You're part of the prophecy. I'd recognize that face anywhere."

You let out an exhausted sigh. "I've been hearing about this *prophecy* thing a lot today," you admit. "What makes you think yours is the real one?"

"Because it's the prophecy they don't want you to know about," the unicorn sneak counters. "Come on. Follow me."

With that, the unicorn creeps along the wall before breaking away and heading out into the grass.

Follow to unicorn to page 48
Decline on page 194

You decide to head after Jorlin, sprinting through the house and erupting out the front door after him. He's already rounded the corner but you hurry along, making your way to the sidewalk and jogging under the streetlights as they cast the scene in their warm glow.

"Hey! Wait up!" you call out.

Jorlin finally slows down and waits for you, an expression of exasperated frustration plastered across his face. "Hey," is all that he offers in return.

"I know you're upset," you start, "but is it *really* worth ending the campaign over? Think of how long we've been running this game for. Think of all the amazing adventures we've had together."

Your friend appears to be unaffected by these pleas. He's made up his mind.

"Yeah, there've been some fun times," Jorlin admits, "but there's *less* every session. I can tell Sarah's getting sick of it, too."

You nod along, just listening for now.

"I'm just tired of Lorbo acting like rules are the only thing that matters," he continues. "Right?"

You hesitate, considering how to play this.

Agree that Lorbo is being a jerk on page 206
Push for finding a balance between the two sides on page 156

You rush toward your blade, sliding across the dirt as the creature lunges over the top of you. Seconds later, your hands find their way around the hilt of your sword, gripping tight as you prepare for the monster's next attack.

The misplacer beast doesn't waste any time, circling back and snarling loudly as it charges again. The creature lashes out with a single tentacle, then follows up with a bite from its enormous jaws.

Fortunately, you're ready. As a long furry appendage shoots in your direction you pull your sword from its sheathe, whipping your blade and slicing the tentacle clean off. Next, you roll to the side, allowing the misplacer beast you drive past you as you take a second swipe with your magic sword.

The creature lets out a howl of agony as you slice it down the middle, the beasts insides spilling forth as it collapses to the ground in a bloody heap.

You wipe the viscera from your weapon, taking a moment to collect yourself. Soon enough, you're resuming your quest.

Your quest continues on page 76

Finally, you nod in agreement. "I accept," you offer. "Let's go see this great wizard."

Melovan the Magnificent smiles, a wave of relief washing over his expression as he gathers up his wands and closes down the shop. Potential customers groan with disappointment, but the bigfoot doesn't seem to care, there's much more at stake here than a few missed sales.

Soon enough, the two of you are weaving your way through the city streets, leaving behind the noise and chaos of the market and gradually drifting back toward the central castle.

Unlike your last trip, however, you don't head toward the front gates. Instead, Melovan leads you around to the side of this massive structure, focused on one of the corner towers. This particular spire is home to Grimble the Grey, another bigfoot wizard who is known for his light fur coat and his incredible arcane skills.

Melovan leads you inside, making your way past the guards and then winding your way up a tightly wound staircase. It feels as though your ascent will never end, like this is some kind of terrible prank to see how long it takes for a set of lungs to explode with exhaustion.

Finally, however, you step out into a beautiful circular room. The place is piled high with various magical items and spell components, a wizard's workshop unlike anything you could've imagined. Beyond this clutter is an endless row of slit windows, each one of them offering an incredible view of the kingdom below.

"Sir!" Melovan blurts, a powerful urgency in his voice as the two of you enter the room. "I have someone I think you should meet."

Standing before their bookshelf is an enormous bigfoot in grey robes and toned similar fur. Grimble places the book he was holding back on the shelf, then slowly turns to greet you. "And who might this be?" he questions.

"I believe they are *the one,*" Melovan the Magnificent continues. "I've never seen such natural magical talent. This is who the prophecy speaks of."

Grimble strolls toward you, looking you over skeptically. He seems quite unconvinced by your presence, but in the spirit of due diligence the bigfoot waves his hand before you.

"Let's see what kind of aura we have then," the grey wizard continues.

A green glow suddenly erupts around your body, causing the bigfoot to jump back in alarm. He stumbles a bit, nearly toppling over a table of tinctures and spell components before regaining his composure.

"Oh my god," Grimble blubbers in amazement, the words tumbling forth as he takes you in with wonder and awe. "The great role-player!"

By the time your aura fades his attitude has changed completely.

"You really *are* the one," Grimble the Grey admits with a solemn nod. He glances over and excuses Melovan, then returns to his bookshelf and pulls out a thick, ancient tome.

Grimble approaches you with this massive book and drops it on the table before you with a loud thud. He opens it up, flipping through the old yellowing pages until finally arriving at the section he's looking for.

An image of another wizard's tower has been sketched upon the parchment below you, this building a dark and twisted reflection of the spire you currently stand in. There's something about its architecture that's undeniably wicked.

"An evil sorcerer at the edge of our world has discovered a new source of arcane power," Grimble explains. "His name is Count Storb. No longer content with the necromantic energy of life and death, he has harnessed the eternal cosmic emptiness of The Void itself."

"The black ooze," you reply with a nod.

"Yes," Grimble confirms. "This substance is bad enough on its own, but when combined with the creatures of our land, it has created all kinds of monstruous abominations. The fearsome beasts of our world are becoming more and more powerful, and soon enough the forces of good will no longer be able to push them back."

"How can we stop him?" you question.

"How can *you* stop him," Grimble corrects. "You are the one this prophecy speaks of, so the power is yours. It's up to you to travel to the dark wizard's tower and slay him dead."

"Oh," you stammer, suddenly feeling awkward about the task at hand. "Like… kill him?"

Grimble senses your hesitation. "I mean... if that's a problem for you, ethically speaking, you could just turn him into a frog."

You consider your mission a moment, still not entirely convinced this is the right path. It sounds quite thrilling, that's for sure, but

214

dispatching an evil wizard is a lot to ask.

Accept the mission on page 189
Decline the mission on page 69

Obviously, the rules are important," you start, choosing your words carefully, "but that's not all there is to it. It's about finding the right balance, don't you think?"

Lorbo scoffs. "Balance is subjective. I think Jorlin and I each have our own idea of where that middle ground lies."

"There's gotta be some crossover," you reply. "I'll be real with you, you'll have to compromise a bit, but Jorlin will, too. This game has been running way too long for it to fall apart over some silly argument."

Lorbo quiets down, allowing your words to sink in as he picks up another small rock in his hands. He eyes a large tree at the far end of the yard, it's thick trunk barely visible to us in the dim light of this cool spring evening.

Lorbo rolls the stone around in his palm, adjusting to the weight and then finally hurling it at his target. It's too dark to see the rock's trajectory, but there's a hollow crack as it bounces off bark and drops into the garden below.

"What do _you_ know about balance anyway?" Lorbo jokes. "I bet you couldn't hit that tree from here."

"What are we betting on?" you question.

Lorbo smiles. "If you can throw a pebble and hit that tree, I'll apologize to Jorlin."

You laugh. "Doesn't sound like a very sincere apology."

Your friend shrugs. "Take it or leave it. I'm giving you a chance here."

"Fine," you reply, taking a deep breath and centering yourself.

Unlike Lorbo, whose aim is solid enough to throw while sitting down, you select your rock and stand up. You take a moment to find the correct stance, then picture yourself hurling this stone toward its intended target.

There's typically a slight hook to your throw, so you adjust accordingly. As you imagine the toss, you find your aim cheating just barely to the side of your target.

You give yourself a fifty-fifty chance of hitting your mark, then consider which side to err on.

Aim a little to the left on page 63
Aim a little to the right on page 204

Before this massive guard dog has a chance to get any more riled up, you reveal your piping hot plate of spaghetti. Immediately, the savage beast's expression transforms from one of threatening rage to unfiltered love and appreciation.

You carefully set the *SPAGHETTI* down between you and the canine, watching as the pup approaches happily and dives in. Soon enough, the dog is lapping away at this unexpected treat, wagging his tail as he devours the evening snack.

As the pup is distracted, you creep your way past him and continue down the hall.

Soon enough, you find yourself standing outside King Rolo's chambers. You can hear the sentient twenty-sided die snoring away within, and as you slowly push open the door you catch sight of him on the far side of the room. The king drifting in a deep sleep, his eyes shut tight as he rests upon his throne.

You remember this room quite well, but upon this second visit you're much more aware of the secret nooks and crannies. You make a hard left turn after entering, creeping over to an inconspicuous iron door and slipping within.

This is the king's royal closet, a large room packed full of beautiful, ornate robes that are constructed from the kingdom's finest materials. Any one of these luxurious garments would fetch a hefty sum on the open market, but right now your sights are set on something much more valuable.

Dropping to your knees, you slide a handful of robes to the side and reveal a large safe built directly into the stone wall.

Now comes the difficult part.

Thanks to some pilfered blueprints, you knew this is where the safe would be located. You also knew it would be equipped with a lock, and that you'd open the lock by answering a very difficult question.

It is said this question would be a *nearly impossible* calculation, one that has plagued mankind for ages.

There is a sentence carved deep into the face of this metal safe, and you read it aloud to yourself.

"Your roll is 11, your THAC0 is 10, their armor class is -2," you recite under your breath.

Below this phrase are two clearly labeled buttons, one says 'hit' and the other says 'miss'.

Press the button marked 'hit' on page 117
Press the button marked 'miss' on page 185

"Yes, of course," you reply. "I still carry it with me."

Lady Norbalo smiles, then extends her hand. "It's time you received a proper blade."

You remove your *DAGGER* a place it gently in the unicorn's palm. Lady Norbalo takes the blade, then reaches back to draw forth a beautiful BLUE SWORD.

You can't help but gasp when you see this powerful weapon, shocked by the sparkling magical energy that courses through it. The unicorn places it into your hand, and as your fingers close tight around the hilt you can feel a pulse of arcane power surge through you.

"Crafted by the finest blacksmith in Billings, then enchanted by a master wizard," the unicorn explains. "This blade should guide you well."

While a longer graduation ceremony might be nice, there's little time to waste now that your training is complete. The darkness grows more and more every day, and now it's up to you to stop it.

Soon enough, you're heading out through the city gates, finding yourself in the beautiful rolling fields of yellow grass that surround Billings. The sight is absolutely majestic, and although you've taken in this landscape plenty of times before, you can't help but give this glorious golden vision some extra weight within your mind. The adventure that lies ahead is a dangerous one, and there's a good chance you may never see these fields again.

According to Lady Norbalo the dragon is located due North, which means you won't have the comfort of a dirt road for the majority of your trek. You'll be stuck walking directly through the rolling grass for quite some time.

Without a moment's hesitation, you head off into the open fields, cutting a straight line across these wide open plains.

The city grows smaller behind you as the sun creeps its way across the sky. You walk for hours, then gradually come to rest under the shade of an old gnarled tree that has sprung up as a singular landmark across this vacant landscape. Out here, the grass is even taller than before, grown so high that you can barely see over the top of it.

Exhausted from the morning hike, you sit down on one of the tree's large roots, reaching back and opening your traveler's pack. You're searching for the lunch you brought along, but it quickly becomes apparent your food has been misplaced.

You could've sworn you packed it, you think to yourself, a certainty so potent that it actually causes a spark of alarm to ignite within you. There's no way you could've naturally misplaced your lunch.

Suddenly, an enormous misplacer beast leaps at you from the tall grass.

Dodge to the left on page 12
Dodge to the right on page 47

There's something about the open wilds that calls to you, the simmering promise of adventure that you just can't find within the safety of these city walls.

You turn right and head toward the main gates, making your way through them and immediately finding yourself in a beautiful landscape of golden grass. The wind rustles across these wide open hills in gentle waves, creating a breathtaking vista that stretches out before you.

You continue walking, making your way down the road that slices across these rolling plains. Eventually, you crest a hill to find a lone figure sitting peacefully on the side of the lane, perched on the edge of a crumbling stone wall.

They wave excitedly when they see you, acting as though they've been long expecting you to pass by, but you don't think you've ever seen this person before in your life. You'd certainly remember it if you did.

The figure wears a stark white robe and sports a pink cloth bag over the top of their head. The words 'love is real' are scrawled across the front of this bag, and their eyes are covered by strange goggles featuring dark, smokey glass that obscures any clue to their identity.

"Hey there, buckaroo," the figure calls out as you continue your approach.

"Oh, hi," you reply awkwardly.

"Looks like you're searching for some direction," the figure offers.

Technically, this is a question, but the mysterious man says it with an unusual amount of certainty in his voice. It's enough to give you pause, wondering just what kind of unknown sorcery is at play.

"Who are you?" you question.

"True buckaroo Chuck Tingle," the man on the wall explains. "I'm here to help you find a path of non-violence. I know you've got this big prophecy to take care of and I know you've decided to say 'no swords buddy!' which is pretty neat."

"I just don't think being a warrior is my calling," you admit.

Chuck leans in a little, lowering his voice as though he's letting you in on some powerful cosmic secret. "Gonna be honest bud, fightin' and stabbin' is bad news outside of books, but you shouldn't feel too bad about doin' it in here. This is a way of fiction so no buds are actually gettin' hurt. That trot said, it is also dang fun to find another option, so I will help you in this way," he explains. "True buckaroo path is way of trottin' inward, so while everyone else is off slayin' dragons and kissin' sorcerers we gotta find way to save the kingdom without all that. Sometimes best way to battle darkness is through love."

"That's true," you admit with a nod.

Chuck hops down from his spot on the wall. "What do you say, bud? Wanna come save the dang world?"

Follow Chuck to page 126
Decline on page 209

You gradually begin to position yourself in front of the column, evading the troll's attacks and waiting until the creature takes a powerful lunge.

The monster barrels toward you in a rage, taking a massive, wild swipe with his powerful claw. You've been waiting for this moment, tracking the movement of his long green arm from beginning to end as you duck below and spring out of the way.

The troll strikes the post behind you, blasting through heavy stone and immediately causing the ceiling to cascade down. The monster cries out in shock, raising his hands to protect himself but unable to avoid the massive stone bricks that slam his body the floor and crush him under their weight in a plume of dust.

When the haze clears, very little of the troll is left to stick out from under the rubble, only an arm and the top of his brutally crushed skull. Dark green blood slowly begins to leak out from beneath the stone, pooling around the wreckage.

You did it, you suddenly realize. Your first warriors task is complete.

You approach what's left of the troll's body, leaning down and pulling off a large patch of the beast's stringy black hard as evidence of your victory.

The second you're finished, you turn and make your way back up to the world above. You don't wanna stay in this putrid chamber one second longer than you have to, and you're ready to continue your training with Lady Norbalo.

Return victorious to page 33

"It's your brother!" you cry. "They were attacked by a band of ruthless coblins and now they're clinging to life. Go! Be with your family in this time of need!"

The stegosaurus nods profusely, her panic growing. "But what of the castle? It's my duty to guard."

"I've been assigned to your post," you continue. "Now go!"

The dinosaur turns to leave and you immediately relax, thankful your little story has managed to carry you this far. So much of the plan is riding on this moment, and you're thrilled to discover that it actually worked.

The second you drop your guard, however, disaster strikes.

The stegosaurus turns for a split second, feigning as though she's about to run. Instead, however, she uses this as an opportunity to quickly unsheathe her sword.

The dinosaur twirls around and lashes out with her weapon, swiping it across your neck and causing an eruption of blood to spray forth. Your head is not completely severed, but it might as well be.

You drop to your knees before the castle, gasping for air and gazing up at the stegosaurus.

"I don't have a brother," she offers as you collapse in a heap, your vision fading to black.

THE END

"I'm sorry," you finally announce, standing up from the table. "I don't think this mission is for me."

The sentient book just stares at you for a moment, a great sorrow in her eyes. You expect her to be disappointment, and she certainly is, but the emotion that floods her gaze is much more complicated.

"Are you sure?" Darba questions. "Think wisely on how you answer."

You consider her words for a moment, but finally decide that staying true to yourself is the only choice. You don't want to steal from the king, it's as simple as that.

"I'm sure," you offer, turning to exit the chamber when you suddenly feel a sharp pang in your stomach. A figure clad in a dark assassin's robe wraps their arms around you and pulls you close, pushing their blade even deeper into your belly.

"I just..." you stammer, then find your words coming out in a strange coughing gurgle.

Seconds later, the assassin releases their grip and slips back into the shadows. You stagger toward the door but your body feels too heavy to move, disobeying the commands of your mind as you struggle to stay upright.

Your knees buckle as you collapse to the cold stone floor, and although your blood is spilling forth at a terrifying rate, you get the sense that the wound itself is the least of your worries.

A powerful burning sensation quickly floods your veins, starting at the pit of your stomach and then working its way through you with feverish intensity. The blade that sliced you open must've been covered with a mighty poison, and even though the end is near, your thankful for this quick release.

You fully collapse to the ground, your face against the floor as you enter a state of numb paralysis. You don't feel anything, and soon enough your vision fades to an endless darkness.

THE END

"No way am I going with you," you reply. "Fulfill the prophecy yourself."

The unicorn is clearly disappointed to hear this, taking a moment to sit with your answer and then letting out a long sigh of acceptance as they come to terms with your denial.

Finally, they nod.

"Nobody can know I was here," they say, then reach into a small bag on their belt.

To your surprise, the unicorn pulls forth a handful of crispy, breaded chicken tenders and throws them into your cell.

"What the hell?" you blurt. "Are these for me?"

The unicorn shakes their head solemnly. "They're for the troll. He'll smell them all the way down in the depths."

With that, your mysterious visitor turns and disappears back into the shadows from which they came.

You stand for a moment, wondering if you've just made a terrible mistake. Eventually, you begin to hear a faint rumbling sound, the pulsing tremors coming from somewhere deep within this stone labyrinth. Louder and louder they get, gradually revealing themselves as thunderous stomping feet.

Suddenly, the iron door next to you flies open and a massive troll drags himself out of the depths. The creature is enormous and disgusting, dripping with slime and smelling of rot.

"Chicken tendies with a side of human!" he cries out as you back away from your cell door.

The troll grabs the bars and gives a solid yank, tearing them from their rusted hinges. This is your only chance of escape, and you take it, but the troll easily grabs you with his long arms and pulls you toward him.

"Human first!" he blubbers excitedly, then opens his jaws to reveal a set of huge, razor sharp teeth.

You try your best to struggle away but the creature is too strong. The troll snaps his gaping maw forward, chomping his teeth around your neck and biting your head clean off.

THE END

Made in the USA
Coppell, TX
05 December 2021

67259993R00128